Mrs Whitelady

Julie Telford

To my brother Berwick, and Rhona. Hope you enjoy it. Julie

Published in 2012 by FeedARead.com Publishing – Arts Council funded

Copyright © Julie Telford

The author or authors assert their moral right under the Copyright, Designs and Patents Act, 1988, to be identified as the author or authors of this work.

All Rights reserved. No part of this publication may be reproduced, copied, stored in a retrieval system, or transmitted, in any form or by any means, without the prior written consent of the copyright holder, nor be otherwise circulated in any form of binding or cover other than that in which it is published and without a similar condition being imposed on the subsequent purchaser.

A CIP catalogue record for this title is available from the British Library.

This is a work of fiction. All names and characters in it are works of the author's imagination. Any resemblance to real persons, living or dead, is entirely coincidental.

Julie Telford was born in Edinburgh in 1952. She now lives in France and has visited Africa many times.

An earlier version of Mrs Whitelady, 'Welcome to Africa, Mrs Bennett' won the Daily Telegraph/Alexander McCall Smith online serialised novel competition in 2009.

The proceeds of this book will go to Oxfam, towards primary education in sub-Saharan Africa.

1

Sunday

It was dark when we got to Wenduzu. My legs trembled as I stepped out of the Land Rover onto solid ground. It had been a long, rough journey: five hours of hairy bends and potholes, and once night fell, total darkness apart from the headlights, which had illuminated some alarming insects thudding into the windscreen. All three of us were drenched in sweat and Annabel and I had been travelsick.

'This is it,' said the driver, his teeth gleaming through the darkness. We were in front of a gate in a high white wall 'Now wait.' He got out of the car and disappeared through the opening.

The headlights shone on a sign: *Wenduzu Provincial Hospital Residential Compound.*

The warm night air fell upon us like a blanket, and a cacophony of screeches, chirrups and howls filled our ears.

'Jungle,' grinned Jeff. He looked excited.

I pondered over what malevolent creatures might be lurking in the darkness. The sooner we were on the other side of that wall, the better, probably. Even so, I wondered what on Earth awaited us.

'Africa, Laura! How do you fancy it?'

We had both just come home from work. Jeff was looking through his mail and I was about to go shopping.

'I'll put it on my list,' I said.

'No, really! Look here.' Jeff thrust the letter with the job offer in front of me, and slid his arms around my waist.

It was a two-year contract at the hospital of a small provincial town in Sub-Saharan Africa, five hundred miles inland from the Indian Ocean.

'So the deepest, darkest part of 'The Dark Continent', then?'

'Yeah, sounds great, doesn't it?' Reading my doubt, he added, 'But not at all dark - light, actually - sunny. Think light therapy, Laura.' Jeff let go of me and moved around the kitchen, opening cupboard doors, looking for snacks.

I had a problem with depression, especially in the winter. My eyes slid to the window. Rain was falling on miserable, congested, polluted London. How could I not want to get away from there? It was October and I had six months of gloom ahead of me. It was tempting to up and go somewhere sunny. I turned to Jeff with a cautious smile. 'We could try it, I suppose.'

Jeff rushed back over and gave me a hug.

I pushed him away. 'But Africa! It's such blighted continent! All that conflict, and poverty. Couldn't we find somewhere else?'

'I know, Laura. It is blighted. But don't you see? That's exactly what makes it worthwhile. We could really make a difference. Are there no peanuts, or anything?'

'You mean, you could. You're a doctor, Jeff. You'd be doing something worthwhile wherever you were. And no, we're cleaned out. I'm just nipping down to the supermarket. Will you stay here with Annabel?'

'OK. But Africa, Laura. Just think...' Jeff started peeling the last few potatoes.

'And what about Annabel? Don't you think it would be irresponsible to take a small child to a place with so many risks? High child mortality for a start, and so much disease, and famine...' I could have gone on - poor sanitation, dangerous insects, snakes, lions... but Jeff interrupted.

'No, not at all, Laura. These things happen to the local people, because they're poor, and they've no clean water.

Professional, salaried expats are insulated from all that. We'll be comfortable, probably very comfortable.'

Jeff's use of 'will' rather than 'would' did not escape my notice, and he knew it, but he had fixed his lovely hazel eyes on mine, willing my consent. He knew more about Africa than I did, anyway. As a medical student he had done an elective on the Kenyan coast. I went to get my coat.

'And now's the right time, Laura, when Annabel's just four, and we don't have to worry about schooling yet'. Jeff started following me downstairs. 'And this is a peaceful place. It's not like Rwanda, or anything.'

'You're staying here with Annabel,' I reminded him. 'I'll be back in ten minutes.'

When I got back, I looked up Jeff's guide to East Africa. The civil unrest in Rwanda and Burundi of the early 1990's was at its height, but Wenduzu was far enough away from that. The book said the country was very poor, but stable and peaceful. While not on the tourist trail, it was a spectacularly beautiful land rich in wildlife, with meandering rivers, savannah plains and forested mountain slopes.

He'd persuaded me. It was an opportunity too good to miss, for the work experience for Jeff, and as a bonus, it would be warm and sunny and exotic. At the weekends we could go on safaris. I would keep a diary, and take lots of photographs. I would take along learning materials and stimulating toys for Annabel, and as long as she had other children to play with, and we looked after her health, she would be all right, hopefully. I would have more time to spend with her, too. I would enjoy that. London life was frantic with us both working full-time.

I hoped I, too, could do something for Africa: tutoring, perhaps, or help at the hospital. Part-time work would be ideal. We could find childcare locally.

But mostly I wanted to please Jeff, my kind, loving, generous husband who wanted to make a difference to the world, and who had worked hard at becoming a doctor so that he could do just that. He deserved this opportunity. I couldn't let him down.

A slender European woman in a white linen dress and pearls emerged from the gate.
'*Karibu*! Welcome! You have arrived safely at last!' As she embraced us I noticed she was wearing expensive perfume. I hoped my own sweaty body was not too offensive.
Sofia told us she was from Milan. She was the hospital paediatrician and wife of Roy, the hospital superintendant.
'You will meet him later. We are holding a welcoming party for you.'
'Bambina bella!' she exclaimed under her breath, as I lifted the sleeping Annabel from the car. We followed her to our new home, a two-bedroom bungalow. I was relieved to see that its furnishings were adequate, if somewhat basic. There was a fridge, thank goodness, a big table, nice wooden floors, and a wooden-framed sofa and armchairs with foam cushions. There was no television – of course – but that was all right. I murmured approval.
'And mosquito nets over the beds,' said Sofia.' Very important!'
'Might there be a phone we could use? I'd like to tell the family we've arrived.'
'No, the phones don't work here. Didn't anyone tell you?'
'They did, but I hoped it wasn't true.'
'It is true.' Sofia threw her hands up as if in exasperation.
She pointed across the courtyard. 'That's our bungalow opposite. Come over when you are ready. We will all be waiting for you.' Then her stiletto heels went click-clack along the path.

I didn't feel like going to the party but Jeff pointed out that this might be our only opportunity to eat that evening. We hadn't brought any food with us. Our luggage allowance had been taken up by everything we would need for our two-year stay, that is, all we would need and couldn't get locally, which was more or less everything - like two years' supply of factor-60 sun-cream. Jeff never burned but Annabel and I had the tender skin that goes with fair hair.

There would be no opportunity to have things sent on to us; we had been told that the country's communication systems, including the postal service and the telephones, were all but dysfunctional.

So, there had been no room for food, apart from some cheese, which had gone sweaty and chocolate, which had now melted.

After showering, we ventured across to Sofia and Roy's bungalow.

'Welcome!' Sofia ushered us in to a room full of people.

'Attention, everybody! Here's our new obstetrician, Doctor Jeff Wittley, his wife Laura, and this beautiful little girl is Annabel.'

Jeff immersed himself in getting to know his new colleagues while I went through the party in a daze, not remembering anyone's name or what they did. Thankfully, there was plenty of focus on Annabel, especially among the women. Our golden-haired daughter seldom failed to attract attention, and as ever, she was a wellspring of delight.

The men talked shop, but their medical jargon was lost on me. I smiled and nodded and stifled yawns, and was relieved when attention was drawn to the food. Sofia had laid on a huge buffet: roast beef, spicy chicken breasts, a honey-roast ham, an impressive array of salads, one had flowers strewn all over it. Were they were meant to be eaten or were they purely decorative?

I was amazed. Where had it all come from, to this place so far from anywhere? I was relieved that it was European food. I was not ready to stomach caterpillars, or whatever.

It was as delicious as it looked. Annabel and I soon got over our carsickness, though not my craving to get into a nice cool bed. But the party had been put on for us, so I had to make an effort. Sofia would have been offended if we hadn't stayed.

She was obviously one of those superwomen who could cope with several things at once and still stay cool. More than cool, she was impeccable: slim, elegant, composed. Her dress was clearly expensive, her dark hair sleek and well-cut, and her made up expertly applied. My clothes were un-ironed, my hair was still wet from the shower, and I hadn't bothered to do my face.

'Are you a doctor, too?' Sofia asked me.

'Me? No - I'm not.'

'What's your profession, then?'

Her question seemed blunt, but I forgave her. The Italians were less restrained than the British.

'Well, I've been working in an office, but here, I suppose....'

'Oh, you could be my secretary, then. I need one.'

'Oh! Er, I'm going to be a full-time mother, for the time being...' I didn't like this interrogation and turned away from her to help myself to a crisp salad with balsamic dressing.

'Mmmm, this is lovely!'

'Looking after children – it's a full-time job – no doubt!'

'You don't have any children?'

'Oh yes! We have four. But they are older. They are all at boarding school.'

'I would like to work. Perhaps I can find someone to look after Annabel...' It came out sounding like an apology.

'But of course you will!'

'I don't know any Swahili yet...' I felt events could be taken out of my hands if I didn't get a grip, but Sofia had already turned to search for someone. 'Edward! Come here!'

A burly middle-aged African emerged from the crowd flashing a big smile.

'Edward, Laura needs someone to look after Annabel. You can help, can't you?'

Edward was the hospital administrator. We had been introduced already, I remembered now.

'Yes – yes. I know someone who would be very suitable,' he nodded vigorously.

'And she wants to learn Swahili. We'll need to find a teacher for her, Edward.'

'Yes, yes, I know someone. She can teach Swahili too. I'll bring her tomorrow.'

'That's great,' I said. I had been thinking along similar lines, although I hadn't expected to get these things fixed up immediately. I had been looking forward to playing with Annabel, teaching her, watching her grow up. I would have to take more control of my own affairs, I noted inwardly, but I was too tired to argue.

As soon as it seemed not too rude, I excused myself and left to put Annabel and myself to bed.

2

Monday

We awoke to a prolonged screeching sound. It was six am and just beginning to get light. Was it a factory whistle, or a wake-up call for the hospital workers? I was appalled at the thought.

Jeff realised first. 'Crickets,' he grinned. 'The dawn chorus.' He leapt out of bed to have a look.

Sleepily, I joined him at the door. We gazed out onto the courtyard. A few bungalows encircled a garden with a small swimming pool at one side. A two-meter-high wall surrounded the enclosure, and a security man guarded the gate. It felt eerily quiet after the hustle and bustle of London. Inside the compound, there was only the sound of the security man whistling, while outside we heard muted chattering of people walking past, trees swishing in the breeze, and some unfamiliar birdsong.

'Listen to that, Laura. I wonder what kind of bird that is. It's exciting, isn't it?'

I nodded. 'No idea about tropical birds. Could be anything. Perhaps it's monkeys.' Whatever it was, there was certainly a lot of activity going on and it struck me that it was not necessarily benign. I was glad of that high wall.

Someone had left us bread and jam and instant coffee for breakfast.

'Will you and Annabel be all right on your own, then,' Jeff asked while we ate.

'Of course,' I said. I supposed we would be. Anyway, I didn't want to burden him with my anxieties on his first day. I told him what I had fixed up with Edward, the administrator.

'That's great, Laura. Seize the day!' With that, Jeff got up to join his colleagues and go to work.

I let Annabel sleep while I started unpacking. She woke an hour later when there was a loud knock at the door.

'*Hodi Hodi?* – Hello!' It was Edward, with a girl who looked about sixteen.

'*Jambo, Mama.* Good morning, Mrs Whiteley. Have you slept well?'

'Very well, thank you,' I told him, truthfully. I didn't correct his mispronunciation of my name.

'This is my daughter, Hope,' he beamed. 'She has just graduated from high school.'

'Pleased to meet you, Hope.' I smiled and shook her hand. I couldn't resist asking, 'Do you have sisters called Faith and Charity?'

'Yes,' she answered demurely.

I didn't tell her I had meant it as a joke. It had been thoughtless of me. I introduced Annabel, who had drowsily wrapped her arms around my legs, then I explained that I wanted someone both as a childminder and a Swahili teacher, offering to pay her one American dollar per morning, as advised by Sofia the night before. Hope's face lit up on hearing this, and put my mind at rest that it wasn't a ridiculously low rate of pay after all.

We all agreed that she should turn up for work at eight the next morning. There didn't seem much point in giving her an interview, or in finding out how well she related to Annabel. All in good time, I thought.

'Now, I think I had better take you to the bank,' said Edward. 'You will need to open an account. I know someone there who can give us priority, otherwise you will be waiting all morning in the queue.'

He was right. Huge numbers of people were waiting to be

served at the bank. Edward told me to sit down and he strode up to the counter and spoke to one of the bank clerks.

A few minutes later he came back smiling. 'Yes, I have explained to my friend. She can see you now.'

Opening an account involved protracted form-filling. After ten minutes, the bank clerk finally declared it completed. 'Now Mrs Whitely, how many shillings would you like for now?

'Wittley,' I corrected her. I had no idea how many shillings I should take. 'Give me five hundred US dollars worth,' I said.

The young woman's face broke into a smile, which she tried not to show. She opened a drawer, pondered a while over the bundles therein, then laid most of them on the counter. Laboriously, she counted out the notes, then she leaned over and spoke to me in a conspiratorial tone. 'There you are, Mrs Whitely, six hundred and thirty-eight thousand, three hundred and forty-one shillings.'

'Thank you,' I said, returning a secretive smile, and stuffed the notes into my purse until it would take no more. I scooped up the rest and dropped them into my shopping bag.

On the way back, Edward pointed out various landmarks. It seemed there was not much to the town, consisting only of a single street of small shops and a few key buildings: the town hall, the police station, a run-down hotel, a couple of churches, and a nunnery, all spread widely over otherwise unused land. There would be no parking problems, I noted - if one had a car, which we did not, and it looked as if we would need one, yet another thing to think about.

'Now, you'll want to buy food. We can stop quickly at the marketplace.' Edward looked at his watch. 'But I don't have much time.'

Someone had put a few basic provisions in our fridge, which would keep us going for a couple of days, but I didn't want to lug shopping the mile or so back by foot. The nausea from the night before had returned, too. Perhaps the party food had not been as good as it had looked, or perhaps it was the water. It was supposed to be drinkable; maybe my stomach just needed to toughen up. I took up Edward's offer. 'Two minutes?'

I grabbed Annabel and opened the door. The heat hit me, and smells of food fast losing its freshness came in waves. I hurried round the stalls. What should I buy? Through the swarms of people I viewed displays of meat and fish covered in flies. Other stalls were piled up with various dried grains and beans. What did one do with those grains? Would I have to pound them? The only other produce I saw were bananas and some fruits and vegetables I didn't recognise. So many things were unfamiliar. So many new things to think of all at once, decisions to make – where did one start? It was all so strange, overwhelming. It felt unreal.

Strange fruit - there was a song about that, wasn't there? A rather disturbing one…

I felt dizzy and sick. *I can't cope with this place.*

I would have to just buy something and get out. I indicated to the stallholder in front of me that I wanted some beans. She filled up an enormous bagful. I didn't try to argue. I pointed to bananas and she handed me a huge bunch. I got out my overstuffed purse and gave her the smallest note I could find. The stallholder burst out laughing. She gestured she would go and look for change.

I thought I might faint. I just wanted to get away. 'Just take it,' I said.

Now everybody was looking at me in amazement, shaking their heads in disapproval. *Those white people – they have far too much money.*

I hurried back to the car, my left arm embracing the loads of beans and bananas, my right hand clutching Annabel tightly.

'Thank you for waiting,' I smiled wanly to Edward. 'I'm very grateful to you.'

When we got back, Annabel and I plunged into the swimming pool. It was blissfully cool. Ah! That was better.

Monday afternoon

We went out to explore our neighbourhood. A dirt track went past the hospital guesthouse, and a water pump where women and children were queuing with buckets. So the village people here had clean water, too. Then they were better off than most Africans, as far as I understood. Even so, they were obviously extremely poor. It didn't look as if they got enough to eat; everyone was so scrawny.

We walked by clusters of mud huts among mango and banana trees. There were people everywhere, and animals - dogs, chickens, goats scrabbling in the dirt.
It reminded me of something, but what? I hadn't been out of Europe. Nowhere in the developed world was like this anymore more. It was like going back in time.
Then I remembered: the Viking Museum in York. They took you in a carriage through a model village of wattle and daub huts, with mannequins in rough-woven garments cooking over outdoor fires, livestock wandering everywhere. The people here wore cotton, not sackcloth, although the children were in rags. But it was the smells that made it real. They came in wafts: smoking wood, dung, bananas, dogs, cooking, sweat, coconuts.
Annabel was not in the least bit perturbed by her new environs. On the contrary, she thoroughly enjoyed all the attention she was attracting from the villagers, especially the children, who escorted us everywhere. I needn't have worried about getting lost.
I was the apprehensive one, having no idea what dangers might lurk. I kept telling myself to relax, everyone was friendly, stop worrying. Nonetheless, I felt vindicated when

we caught sight of the stiff green tail of a monitor lizard, which must have been about three feet long, slithering into the scrub by the wayside. Those reptiles have viscous claws. I grabbed Annabel's arm. 'You know you must never go into the grass,' I warned her.

Monday evening

Jeff was late coming back from the hospital. The sun had set and it was getting darker by the minute. I tried not to worry. I thought about walking down to the hospital to see if there was a problem, but decided not to. If anyone needed to contact me they should know where to find me.

Finally, he arrived around six thirty. 'I expected you much earlier,' I said, unable to conceal the shake in my voice. 'So how did your first day go?'

Jeff collapsed into a chair. 'Exhausting. So many patients. So many problems. You know, you know rural Africa's going to be a whole new ballgame from Europe, or even the Kenyan coast which is pretty developed in comparison. I knew that, so I'd braced myself - but when the reality of it hits you, it's overwhelming.'

'I know,' I said. 'I had a panic attack in the marketplace this morning.'

'Did you?'

'I'm all right now,' I quickly reassured him. I knew that my problems would be minuscule compared with what he would have encountered.

'Tell me about your day,' I said.

'Oh, stillbirths and all that. I don't want to talk about it.' Jeff leaned back and closed his eyes, grimacing. A tear trickled down his cheek.

I swallowed. I hadn't seen him cry very often. It must have been bad. I thought of reminding him that we didn't need to stay, if it was going to be too much, but I resisted. I knew he would never contemplate giving up so easily. He would be angry if I suggested it.

'Would you like a beer?' I asked him.

'Wow! I'd love a beer. Have we got some?'

'Yes, someone left us a few in the fridge.' I got out two and an orange fizzy drink for Annabel.

'Ah, that's just what I needed,' said Jeff. He gulped half of it down straight from the bottle. 'Annabel, you've got bright orange all round your mouth. You look like a clown.'

Annabel laughed and went to sit on her father's lap.

'It's the dye from the drink,' I said. 'Agent Orange. I bet it would never be allowed in Europe.'

'Laura, Agent Orange was a defoliant in the Vietnam War. It killed and maimed people. Let's get things into perspective, shall we?'

'Sorry.'

He smiled an apology. 'I didn't mean to be hurtful.'

'I understand.'

'I know, let's go for a swim.'

'What, in the dark?'

'Why not?'

Tuesday.

My plan was to let Hope and Annabel spend their first morning getting to know each other, while I sat quietly in a corner reading. I had finished unpacking the day before, and after Annabel and I had returned from exploring the neighbourhood, I was exhausted from the heat, culture shock, and the unbroken attention I was having to give my daughter all day. I had been looking forward to spending time with her, but I wasn't used to it. Now I understood what fulltime mothers complained about.

Unfortunately, Hope showed no interest in Annabel. Instead, she picked up *Out of Africa*, the book that I was reading myself, and settled herself down in a chair with it.

'Er ..., I don't think Annabel will let you read a book if you are to keep her company,' I pointed out, but Hope didn't take the hint. She simply sat there and carried on reading.

Annabel tugged on my arm. 'You play with me, Mummy.'

My little girl's angelic blue eyes peered pleadingly through the long golden locks tumbling about her face. Her expression pulled on my heartstrings. I couldn't leave her alone with such an uninterested childminder. This arrangement was not going to work.

'I know, let's all sit at the table, Annabel can draw a picture, and you can teach me Swahili, Hope, - Hope?'

When we were settled at the table, I looked at Hope expectantly. Hope looked back vacantly.

She was just a girl, I reminded myself. I would have to take the lead. 'All right, how do I say Hello?'

Hope seemed to need time to think. '*Dyambo*,' she said, eventually.

'*Dyambo*,' I repeated.

'No, *Dyambo*,' said Hope.

'*Dyambo*.'

Hope laughed and shook her head. '*Dyambo*.'

I sighed. But didn't I know the word for Hello already? It was in our phrasebook.

'*Jambo*,' I said.

'Yes, that's right,' said Hope. '*Dyambo*.'

'Mummy, look at my picture,' said Annabel. She had drawn two figures, one bigger than the other, outside a house. 'That's me,' she said, pointing to the smaller figure.

'Oh. And is the other one Hope?' I asked, optimistically.

'No. It's you. And that's our house. We went home. Hope didn't come.'

3

Thursday

'Not such a bad breakfast,' I thought as I scoured the mini-jar of caviar that Jeff had been too guilty to eat while flying over Mogadishu. I'd had no such scruples myself, and had polished off my own caviar promptly. Maybe if I had already seen how poor the people here were, I, too, would have felt it wrong, even obscene, to indulge in such luxury, but before we arrived in Africa, I hadn't. Now, I felt there was no point in rejecting the second jar. It would be very wrong to waste food. Anyway, I couldn't resist the temptation. It was my last link with somewhere that was not Africa.

There would be no more culinary delights for the foreseeable future. The baggage allowance had prohibited non-essentials, and we were relying on local produce right from the start.

Today, it was boiled beans for lunch and boiled beans for supper. Three days after arriving, I still hadn't managed to get anything more appetizing. Beans and bananas had been the only food at the market that I had recognised, and that had not been covered in flies. I would have to go back and try again.

Annabel seemed to be enjoying her more mundane breakfast of bread and jam. She probably preferred the white, highly processed bread to the rough wholemeal loaves that I used to buy. Here there was no choice. She didn't seem to mind the flies sharing the jam. They distressed me, though, and I swatted them constantly. Germs were everywhere in Africa. Those flies were going to make us all sick. Or perhaps they already had. I was still feeling slightly nauseous.

'What are we doing today, Mummy?'

'Hope's coming again.' I tried to sound bright. Annabel frowned. She had already made it clear that she didn't like her childminder, but she said nothing now and carried on eating.

I got up from the table and opened the door. No one else was around. They had all gone to work.

The security man caught my eye and waved. '*Jambo, Memsabu Whitelady. Habari?*' he called out. Hello, Mrs Whitelady. How are you?

I smiled, and didn't bother to correct him. The villagers seemed to have decided my name was Mrs Whitelady, rather than Wittley, and it seemed appropriate. Either that or *Mama Annabel*, which defined my function exactly.

'*Mzuri. Habari yako, Bwana?*' I already knew the standard reply: 'Good, and how are you, Mister?' I had learned this much Swahili so far, but I would have to learn a lot more if I was to survive these two years and thrive.

Halfway through our first week, I was not at all certain I would survive, let alone thrive. For a start, it was too, too hot. I felt floppy all the time. The swimming pool was the only relief from the heat but the water shrivelled my skin, and the sun burned it, and Annabel's too, despite the factor-60 sun-cream. We couldn't stay in the pool for more than an hour. Then there were the insects. However much repellent I slapped on, the mosquitoes nipped viciously and there was no respite from the flies. Even in the pool I had to watch out for a water-beetle that was evidently out to get me.

I missed European food. Now that I had eaten the caviar, there would be no more luxuries. I had intended to mete out the chocolate and the cheese we'd brought as small daily treats, but we had guzzled the lot in a bout of homesickness.

How was I going to fill my days? Spending the first three days with Annabel had been a lovely change from the office in London, albeit exhausting. Nonetheless, this exotic continent beckoned. There was so much to see and learn about, fascinating people to meet, life-changing experiences to engage in. I would take photographs, but I wanted to contribute something too, help all these needy people; that was the point of coming to Africa. I should not spend the time just entertaining Annabel in the house. She, too, should get an African experience. I had to make plans.

An exchange I'd had with Sofia on the first evening contributed to my restlessness. The contrast between the revved-up Jeff and my dog-tired self must have struck her.

'How did you and Jeff meet?' Sofia had asked me.

I knew what she really meant. *How could someone like Jeff possibly have paired up with someone like you?*

'We met at university,' I told her, getting up to find a distraction because I didn't feel like answering in more detail.

Unlike Jeff, I had never had a high-profile career. I met him in his final year of medical school while I was plodding through a social science degree. Feeling I'd made a bad choice with this course, when Jeff moved to London to do his intern, I had no qualms about dropping out to go with him. Jeff had to work long and hard that year and we saw little of each other. I took an office job to pass the time, and resolved to complete my degree later.

Then Annabel had come along. I kept my office job to make ends meet, but the baby took my energy and if the work offered career opportunities I didn't rise to them. Maybe I could have tried harder. Many women nowadays managed motherhood and career together. Sofia, for example.

How could I make myself useful here? Who should I ask? Becoming Sofia's secretary didn't appeal. She made me uncomfortable and I didn't want her as my boss. Anyway,

I'd had visions of doing something exciting and noble. You could hardly save the world by doing office work. And yet, it was the one thing I could do. Not the archetypical African adventure, but maybe it was a start.

Childcare still had to be sorted out. So far, Hope had shown no aptitude for it, nor for language-teaching. On Tuesday, as on Monday, I had taken control of the lesson, asking Hope merely to answer my questions. She stretched my patience and I had to keep remembering to be more understanding. According to her, there were no Swahili words for shower, or toys, and why should there be, I had to remind myself, if the things themselves didn't exist in her world?

Nonetheless, the girl did not inspire confidence. I wondered whether I could pay her off. But, Hope's father was Jeff's boss. One had to be careful. She couldn't just be sacked.

So what would it mean? A dollar a day for two years? It added up − to five hundred dollars, at least. Her family would have worked it out.

I didn't want to be thought of as a typical colonial-style white boss-lady, who looked upon black people as subordinates at one's disposal. Yet I feared I had already exuded this very image: the English lady, towering head and shoulders above the natives in her wide-brimmed straw hat, long, floaty frock (white for maximum heat-reflection, and more comfortable than trousers), and a parasol to protect her tender skin from the fiery sun.

I decided to give Hope another chance. I needed to go to the market and I didn't want to drag Annabel there and back in the heat. I would leave her with Hope in my absence. The girl was sixteen, and after all, she was the hospital administrator's daughter. Surely she would act responsibly if it was required of her. Anyway, I would be back within an hour.

'I'm going into town,' I said when she arrived. 'Will you look after Annabel, please? Play with her, won't you? And don't let her go outside in bare feet, because of hookworm, you understand? And don't let her play in the grass, because of snakes.'

I felt I had to spell everything out, but it was important. Having read up on the dangers in Africa I was anxious to take every precaution against them.

Hookworm, I had read, *is an extremely dangerous infection because its damage is silent and insidious.* Hundreds of millions of Africans were infected, the book said, commonly by walking barefoot through areas contaminated with faecal matter. The larvae got in through the feet then they travelled through the veins to the lungs and up the trachea. Then they were swallowed, and got into the intestine, where the larvae matured into adult worms. They sucked blood voraciously, causing anaemia and intellectual, cognitive and growth retardation.

The thought of it made me shudder.

I went through my mental checklist of dangers to avoid: hookworm, snakes, monitor lizards...

'And oh, can you swim, Hope?'

Hope shook her head.

'Then don't go in the swimming pool, all right?'

I felt uncomfortable about leaving the two of them. Annabel did not look happy to stay behind with Hope, but I still harboured notions it would work out between them. I steeled myself and waved goodbye cheerily. 'I'll be back soon,' I called, and set off before it became too hot.

'*Shikamoo, Mama!*' the children greeted me, politely, as they queued to fill up their buckets at the water-pump.

'*Shikamoo, watoto*,' I replied, pleased to have recalled the word for "children". They laughed. Then I remembered,

Shikamoo was the way for "inferiors" to greet their "superiors". *Jambo* was the correct word.

I called out *Jambo* many times after that, in reply to all who greeted me: boys playing on the ground with handmade toys, women pounding mealy in huge bowls outside their mud-hut homes, girls balancing enormous gourds full of water on their heads, or great stacks of wood, others carrying babies. Nearly everyone was carrying a great load as they went along the road.

Even a line of children dressed in school uniform walked along in single file, each with a pile of bricks on his or her head. What on Earth were they doing? Was house-building part of the school curriculum?

At either side of this dirt track, men and women tended vegetables in the *shambas*, or rested under the shade of mango trees. They all paid me a great deal of attention as I walked past. I was used to this already. Even on the first day I had discovered that anonymity was not an option.

But I enjoyed the conviviality. It was a refreshing contrast to the impersonal, insular norms of urban England. And the colour, too. It was so different from drab grey Britain. Why did everyone back home wear black and grey so much? The vibrant hues of the women's clothing were so much more pleasing. My heart lifted. I was warming to this place, definitely.

My pace had slowed down to a stroll, and it took me about thirty minutes to reach the centre of Wenduzu town. It was little more than a single street and a food market. Small shops and the occasional makeshift bar lined both sides of the street, which I thought must have been pedestrianised, until I realised there were so few vehicles that it had never really been anything other than a pedestrian precinct – for humans, stray dogs, and the occasional herd of goats. The shops were more like semi-permanent market-stalls, selling everyday necessities. They weren't of much interest to me, apart from the occasional selection of *kangas*, the brightly-coloured drapes that the women wrapped around their bodies.

The heat made me thirsty, so I stopped off at one of the little bars for a fizzy drink. It was a relief to sit down in the shade in the small enclosure. Once my eyes had adjusted to the darkness, other clients became visible: a few men, and a bejewelled teenage girl sitting apart. I felt out of place and I sensed the others were uncomfortable about my presence, that it wasn't a place for white ladies, but as far as I knew there was no other kind of place to have a drink.

The girl didn't look uncomfortable; she sat quietly singing, and every so often she would ostentatiously rearrange herself. What was she doing there? Why wasn't she out carrying water, or stacks of firewood, or a baby, like all the other teenage girls around here?

One of the men got up, and he must have made some gesture to the girl, because she got up promptly and followed him. Then it twigged. Of course.

Feeling even less comfortable after that, I finished my drink quickly, got up, paid and left.

I was enjoying my child-free time. Annabel could be tiresome when she had to walk any distance.

I went across to the market. Surely there was more on offer than the beans and bananas I had come away with on that first frantic visit. This time, I was in control, and I would shop with composure. I greeted the stallholders with smiles. *Jambo, Bwana...Jambo, Mama. Habari* How are you.... *Mzuri* Good, I replied, when they asked in turn, and I meant it. I did feel good. I would settle in. Somehow, it was all going to work out.

There wasn't much choice among the produce. I selected some yams and some plantains, or cooking bananas, and was pleased to discover I was able to ask the prices, and understand the answers.

Getting out my purse, I caught a glimpse of my watch. Oh my God! I had been away well over an hour. I would have to rush.

I was breathless when I got back. 'Hello-o,' I called out on entering the house.

There was no answer, but Annabel's shoes were by the door, so I knew they were at home, having told Hope not to let Annabel go barefoot, because of hookworm.

'Hello-o.' I looked in every room. The house was empty. This was puzzling. Surely the girl would not let...

Then I remembered my reservations about Hope. Maybe she would let Annabel go out without her shoes on; and, could it be that she was not even supervising her? *Oh my god!*

I dashed out, then dashed back to pick up the shoes. Then I remembered the swimming-pool. *Oh my god!* I dropped the shoes again and hurried over to the pool.

4

My tiny little girl was right in the middle of the swimming-pool, doggy-paddling in water that was two metres deep.

'Annabel!' I shrieked.

'Hallo, Mummy.' Annabel doggy-paddled over to meet me.

'What are you doing in the swimming-pool? It's not safe!'

'But I've got my armbands on.'

She did indeed have armbands on, but seeing this did not abate my anger.

'Even so! It's not safe! What if you had got into difficulties? Hope can't swim. You could have drowned!'

'But I didn't.'

'But you might have; you could have!'

'But I didn't!'

I heard laughter. I turned and saw Hope sitting by the edge of the pool, laughing, with *Out of Africa* in her lap. She was not facing in Annabel's direction. I glared at her, speechless. How could she be so irresponsible!

I found my voice. 'Hope, I told you not to come to the pool because you said you can't swim.' I felt tense and flushed, but noticed that I had automatically lowered my voice and assumed the normal polite tone I used with unfamiliar adults. I was annoyed with myself for doing so, because the blame lay with Hope far more than with the four-year-old. I was more annoyed still when Hope responded by shrugging her shoulders.

'And I see you let her come out in bare feet. I told you not to, because of hookworm,' I continued, more tersely.

Then I noticed that Hope herself was not wearing shoes, and it occurred to me that perhaps she never did. Perhaps she didn't have any.

But why not? Could her family really not afford them? Her father had a job. Didn't they care about their health? Didn't they know the risks?

I felt exasperated, guilty and confused all at once. I wanted Hope to go. I opened my purse and took out two dollars. 'Look, take two days' pay and have a day off tomorrow. I won't be needing you.'

'Thank you, ma'am.' She looked pleasantly surprised as she took the money.

I wished I had sacked her.

Thursday Lunchtime

'I am appalled at her negligence,' I said to Jeff over our lunch of boiled beans. 'I mean, surely a sixteen-year-old should know better. She wasn't looking after Annabel at all.'

'I don't think they have the same concept of looking after small children here. When you look around, the kids are all out playing, or just hanging about, and nobody's really looking after them. And the adults are just getting on with their work.'

'I suppose you're right. Nobody really watched over us, when we were small, now that I think about it. The kids all looked out for each other, or, at least, it was assumed that they would. I don't suppose it was even a conscious decision. But there were always plenty of kids around; that's the difference, and no swimming pools!'

'There were other dangers, though, weren't there? The vigilance has been an after-thought, in the rich world.'

'So, OK, maybe she was just acting normally for her culture, but it's not our culture, and I'm sorry, but I'm not prepared to assimilate to that extent, not as far as to take risks like that.'

'Of course not.'

'But what do we do? Should I sack Hope, or would that involve complications, especially with Hope's father being your boss?'

'Edward is not my boss,' said Jeff. 'I'm a consultant and he's just the administrator. He pays my wages and so on.'

'Well, exactly.'

'I don't know, Laura. I can't think about things like that on top of everything else I have to cope with. Two women died in childbirth, this morning.'

I gasped. 'Two? But that's awful! How come?'

'It's awful, but it's not surprising, given the statistics. We can expect to get two or three women dying in childbirth every week at this hospital.

'But it's a good hospital. It has good well-trained doctors, like yourself...'

'Good for Africa, probably. The trouble is they don't come to hospital to give birth, and we couldn't possibly cope with all of them if they did – we just don't have the resources. They have their babies at home, with an untrained midwife, and they only come to the hospital when they get complications, as a last resort – the women themselves don't get a say in it; their men decide – and sometimes it's too late. One of the deaths today was the result of a botched abortion, and the other woman who died had AIDS. That's nothing unusual.'

Jeff sighed and closed his eyes. I knew how harrowing it would be for him. It certainly put my own problems into perspective.

'Anyway, I've got to get back. By the way, Sofia and Roy have invited us over for dinner again tonight.'

'Oh, that's nice,' I said with relief. 'Because it was going to be boiled beans again for supper.'

Thursday Afternoon

'Let's go for a little walk,' I said to Annabel after our siesta. I needed to regain some composure.

Annabel was pleased to go because she was popular with the village children. She was the only white child around, and indisputably, a very charming one. She was only too happy to play the role of idol.

The problem of Hope plagued me. I hated the idea of getting on the wrong side of anybody so soon, especially in an unfamiliar place where I wouldn't be aware of the consequences. If I did dismiss her, I would need to find another minder for Annabel, if I wanted to work. Would I find anyone better? There was no guarantee. There was no such thing as common sense, I had read in a sociology textbook. Rather, the knowledge we internalise is culture dependent. So, what would an ex-high-school girl in a small town in Africa know about swimming pools? And in a place where everyone went around barefoot, how would they understand the importance of wearing shoes? We forget how narrow our own little world is, and fail to realise that things are different elsewhere. This was why travel broadened the mind. You discovered how big and diverse the world was, and how small and narrow-minded and ignorant and unimportant the individual was in comparison.

Such were my musings as we set off on our walk, but they were soon interrupted. As we approached the hospital guesthouse a flashy white Land Cruiser pulled up in front of it, the driver got out and he hurried round to open the passenger door.

A crowd of children materialised from nowhere and headed towards the car just as a white man stepped out of it. A Very Important Person, I guessed.

But the children ran straight past the VIP and rushed on towards to the two of us. 'Annabel! Annabel!' they shouted.

Annabel shrieked in delight and ran to meet them. They seized her hands and they all danced round in a circle.

What wonderful warm spontaneous children! One would never get an experience like that in England, where people were so reserved and cynical and world-weary, even children, I thought.

When the excitement died down one of the boys showed Annabel his handmade motorbike. It had been made from scraps of rubbish: an AA battery for its engine, twisted wire for the frame, sections of mango-stone for the wheels, dried banana-skin for the saddle, and it was tied to a long stick for pushing it along. It was an exquisite work of ingenuity. They let Annabel try it out.

But her eye was drawn to something one of the girls had. It was the head of a doll, a white one with long blonde hair. One of its eyes was missing. It looked in a sorry state, yet the girl was brushing its hair lovingly.

I decided to wait there and let Annabel play with the boys and girls. She was clearly happy to have playmates, and indeed she should have some. It seemed that these children already looked upon Annabel as a close friend.

Stretching my scant knowledge of Swahili I asked the children their names and how old they were. I was surprised by the answers. They were all much older than they looked.

It was uncomfortable standing there in the heat, and I kept having to tell Annabel not to sit on the dirt track. This annoyed her. She wanted to be like the other children.

'Come and play with Annabel tomorrow,' I told them. 'Come to our house.'

I didn't understand the words of their response but the meaning was clear. They had understood. They said they certainly would come, and yes, they knew where Annabel's house was.

Walking past the guesthouse again, I noticed the driver of the Land Cruiser hand over a large coolbox to Sofia. I approached her. I needed to ask if Annabel was also invited to dinner, because if not, I wouldn't be able to go.

She looked amazed. 'But don't you have childcare? What about the girl?'

I explained about it not working out.

'Oh, then of course she should come. Freda and Doris can look after her in the kitchen.'

I would have liked to talk to her. I wanted information on all sorts of things, like childcare, the secretarial job she had mentioned, where to get food. But she was walking quickly towards her house as she spoke, clearly too busy to hang around and chat.

I took Annabel for another swim. This time, I only half-inflated her armbands. After what had happened that morning, the quicker she learned to swim, the better.

5

Thursday Evening

We were pleased to find that all the other residents of the compound had also been invited to the dinner. Thomas, the surgeon occupied one of the five-bedroom bungalows, as he had a wife and six children, who, for one reason and another, after six months, had still not yet managed to join him. Sofia and Roy had the other large bungalow, as they had four older children, all at boarding school. We occupied one of three two-bedroom bungalows, Philippe, the gynaecologist was in another, and Livingstone and Jared, two junior doctors from the north of the country had the third.

Sofia and Roy's house was more like a Roman villa than a bungalow. The rooms were arranged around an open-air atrium for maximum ventilation. The dining-room, or rather, hall, was open to the atrium, its other three walls supporting some imposing, intricately-carved wooden artefacts. A large, solid, mahogany table dominated the room.

On my left at the table was Thomas, a huge Nigerian who laughed loudly and smiled a lot. I warmed immediately to this charming man. I had never met anyone so exuberant and laidback. He kept uttering '*Hakuna matata*', which, I discovered, was not a Nigerian expression but Swahili for 'No worries.'

Philippe was on my right. He was French, a widower, he told me, and he was looking forward to retiring soon. 'It is so difficult for a man to be a gynaecologist here. The women, they are so shy. I have to let my juniors do the examinations.' He looked old and frail. I wondered if he was lonely. 'Will you go back to France, then?' I asked him.

He pondered. 'I don't know. Perhaps. It has been a very long time. I don't know that I could get used to France again.'

I felt sorry for him and resolved to befriend him.

The guest of honour was the VIP who had arrived at the guesthouse that afternoon, a Mr Wilfred Dormley-Glese, the country's representative for the Overseas Development Agency. Sofia had him sitting next to her husband who was leaning into the man's face, rudely, I thought. Jeff had told me earlier that he had overheard Roy give visitor a mouthful on how under-resourced the hospital was. Now he was delivering another tirade about the appalling state of Africa. 'Life expectancy has plummeted below forty! Forty! ... it is the legacy of colonialism ... Africa is a shackled continent ... it is white man's burden and we should pick up the tab...'

The dignitary looked cowered beside the hospital superintendant. 'I quite agree ... the situation is very difficult ... it requires patience ... but you know, we are seeing economic growth at last....'. He came over as a gentle, well-bred man and I didn't think he deserved this kind of bullying. He didn't seem the most influential of policy-makers, however. Perhaps it was not so surprising that he was here. Wasn't a small, poor, beleaguered state in the middle of nowhere the very place to dump a less-able civil servant?

Roy spoke with the hard, no-nonsense accent typical of the East Midlands. He was barely middle-aged but his deeply lined brow betrayed a troubled man. No wonder. He had the responsibility for all the health problems of a provincial town, and the resources for dealing with them were hopelessly inadequate.

Roy seemed so different from his wife. Sofia was ultra-cool, not exactly laidback, but the coping type. This elegant and well-dressed Italian seemed so super-efficient she could just snap her fingers and everything would fall into place. Maybe she should have been the hospital superintendant.

She certainly excelled at catering. She had prepared yet another spectacular dinner. Where had she got all that amazing food, I wondered? Quails' eggs, for example!

Sofia had placed Jeff next to herself, and she was telling him of a time they had gone camping, and in the night a lion had come sniffing around their tent.

'You know Roy, he was all for sounding the alarm, and I had to hold him down, and signal to him to keep very still and calm and just wait. I hardly dared to breathe! And it stayed for, it seemed like, forever!'

Jeff was enthralled. 'And what happened? Did it go away?'

'Oh yes, of course it did eventually,' said Sofia, indifferently.

I would have died.

After the smoked salmon I got up from the table and went to check on Annabel. The servants were looking after her in the kitchen. She was tucking in to an enormous sundae, oblivious to Sofia, who was buzzing around issuing directions to her staff. How many did she have? I counted at least three until she interrupted me.

'Ah, Laura! Such a charming child you have! And how are you settling in? Not without difficulties, I imagine?'

'Just a few. Where to get food, for example. I've hardly come across anything other than beans and bananas at the market. How do you manage to serve up such wonderful meals?'

'Oh, but there's lots at the market. But you have to get there early, around six.'

My jaw dropped. 'Six! In the morning?'

'And there are people around who can sell you things. I must introduce you,' she went on airily. 'And, you know, you can always keep chickens.'

'Hmm, I'd appreciate some guidance...'

'It's unfortunate there are no other women around. But you never know, Thomas's wife might show up one day.' She rolled her eyes. Then she moved in closer and whispered, 'But you know what Nigerians are like.'

I didn't know any Nigerians but I knew they had a reputation for being unreliable, if not universally downright criminal. A Nigerian surgeon, which Thomas was, might be especially worrying, because there were all those stories about how, if you went into a Nigerian hospital for an operation, you got more surgery than you bargained for, and you came out with one kidney less. Meanwhile the surgeon would be running a lucrative business in human organs on the side. Even so, I couldn't imagine this of the lovely man sitting next to me.

'We mustn't paint them all with the same brush,' I murmured, but Sofia was already issuing orders about the next course.

The next course was guinea fowl: *Faraona al Cognac e Mascarpone*. The conversations around the table became louder and more relaxed as the wine flowed. Sofia had settled herself once again next to Jeff and I could no longer hear what she was saying to him, but they seemed to be getting on swimmingly well. Was she wooing my husband?

Perhaps Philippe next to me had read my thoughts. 'You must come and visit me sometime soon,' he said, 'when you are free, when you don't have the little girl.'

So, having a small child affected not only one's ability to work but one's social life too.

Thomas, on my left, must have been listening. He let out a loud laugh, which seemed inappropriate.

'Yes, I'd like to,' I replied to Philippe.

We made our exit before coffee. Annabel had sleepily curled herself into my lap, and the conversation had moved on to the ubiquitous AIDS and its consequences, something a child might well find disturbing.

'Thank you so much for a wonderful evening,' I said to Sofia, 'And for accommodating Annabel. It was so very kind of you…'

'Oh,' said Sofia. 'I meant to mention the nunnery – do you know it? They run a kindergarten. You should try it.'

'Oh! Right,' I said, then added, 'Oh, but we're not Catholics.'

'Oh, I'm sure that won't matter.'

Once Sofia had closed the door, Jeff burst out laughing. 'Since when did not being a Catholic not matter to a Catholic?'

'Well, it's worth a try,' I said. 'It can't make much difference at that age.'

'You wish!'

6

Friday

I had a hangover the next day, having drunk too much of Sofia's delicious wine. At least I didn't have to contend with Hope, having given her the day off.

At least, I thought I had. So why was she turning up now?

Irritated, I got up to greet the girl. 'Hello, I thought I'd...'

Then I saw that the woman who had just come was not Hope. 'Hello. – *Jambo*. Who are you?

'Mary.'

Mary was carrying a mop and broom. So she was the housemaid. I hadn't known I had one, nor did I understand why Mary hadn't come before now.

But there were many things I didn't understand about this place, and my Swahili was not up to asking for an explanation, so I let Mary get on with cleaning the house.

'Mummy, when are the girls and boys coming?'

Of course! I had forgotten all about inviting the village children to play with Annabel. They were probably waiting at the gate already.

They were indeed: a huge number of them – far more than I had invited the previous day. The arrival of Annabel in the village must have been a very exciting event for them.

I couldn't possibly invite them all in. 'Choose just six,' I told her. 'We'll have to turn the others away. They are far too many.'

I had reservations about bringing even six into the house. Would they behave badly, perhaps steal things, bring in contagions?

45

But I had my principles: there would be no Apartheid in our house, and anyway, Annabel needed playmates.

I looked on uncomfortably as my daughter smugly selected six children and closed the gate on the others. The African experience was going to spoil her.

My fears about the children were not groundless. They were boisterous and descended upon the toys as if they had never seen such wonderful items before, and perhaps they hadn't. They were clumsy with them; they didn't seem to realise that they could break, and that they needed to be looked after, so that they could be used another time.

Nor did the housemaid, it seemed. Mary was sweeping myriad little bits of Fuzzy-felt Fantasy Garden into the yard with oblivion. I wished I could explain to her why she shouldn't, but my Swahili wasn't up to it.

Mary was saying something to me. But her words puzzled me, because if I was understanding them correctly, they contradicted her smiling face.

'*Mtoto wangu amekufa,*' I echoed.

'*Ndiyo*'. Yes.

'You mean – do you mean – your baby has died?'

'*Ndiyo*'. Mary resumed her sweeping.

I stood there and stared at her.

'When? How? Why?' I asked in English.

Mary simply repeated '*Ndiyo*', and carried on sweeping.

I then remembered a conversation at dinner the night before. There had been a consensus that it wasn't polite to ask why someone had died. It was very often because of AIDS, and no-one liked to talk about that.

My Swahili was severely lacking, but still, I felt I knew the correct thing to say now. '*Pole sana*'. I am so sorry.

'This is crazy,' I thought, as I fizzed up a phial of vitamin tablets. I had bought them in England, and I had just worked out that they had cost the equivalent of a week's wages at local rates. Why were these children so under-nourished, when there were vitamins growing all around? There were bananas, mangos - ok, the mangos weren't ripe yet, but, maize, and pineapples surely – certainly bananas. The children were bone-thin, and they looked and behaved a lot younger than their years. I had asked them their ages the day before. Keni was ten but looked seven. He ran to the other side of the yard when Annabel showed him her magnetic letter set. Salome was fourteen but she looked about ten. She was playing with a doll. Miki was eighteen but seemed more like a small fourteen-year-old. He appeared to be challenged by a game 'for ages 4-7'.

Would malnourishment slow their mental development too, I wondered as I handed out the drinks. Or was it a lack of education? Why were they not in school, anyway? I went to get a Swahili dictionary to work out how to ask them. I also wanted to tell them to stop eating the play-dough.

I came back to a flurry of excitement. A boy named Joffre had somehow evaded security and had come in with a monkey. They fell out of the trees sometimes, I had heard. The children were teasing it mercilessly, throwing stones at it, and it had run into a corner.

'Stop it!' I yelled in English. My heart went out to the miserable, cowering creature. 'Let's give it a banana.'

I fetched one from the fridge and held it out. The monkey approached cautiously, freezing every few steps to reassess the situation. Finally it dashed forward, grabbed the banana and scampered back to its corner. The children laughed and resumed their stone-chucking.

I sighed. What was the point in feeling sorry for it? It was probably going to end up in a cooking pot.

The children clearly loved the fizzy yellow drink and now they were holding their cups out for more.

'Pole sana', I told them. Very sorry. The rest of the vitamin tablets had to last a long time.

I picked up the dictionary again but it was too late to tell them not to eat the play-dough. I was glad, in a way. It would have seemed so unfriendly.

'Why – you not go – school?' I finally formulated my question with the aid of the Swahili dictionary.

The children stared back at me blankly.

'You not go school. Why?' I reformulated.

The children continued to stare.

'Why not school?'

They remained silent.

I tried the other word for school in the dictionary. *'Shule'*.

Then Miki, who was eighteen and therefore, no doubt, felt himself exempt from the accusation, said something to the others, and a wave of enlightenment swept over their faces.

'*Shool*,' they echoed my obviously wrong pronunciation, and collapsed about themselves, laughing.

When they stopped, Miki said something I didn't catch, and it was my turn to look blank.

Then he said something else, and I thought I caught 'twenty thousand shillings.'

Of course! It was the school fees. They couldn't afford them.

Now, twenty thousand shillings was not very much in European terms. We could pay for the lot of them and it wouldn't make much of a dent in our budget. So should we?

The children seemed to read my thoughts and they looked up at me hopefully.

Yet, if them, then why not the others outside, too? Perhaps there were hundreds of children whose parents couldn't afford the school fees – or thousands, or more. What was the extent of the problem? Roy had gone on about such problems at great length to the Development Agency official the night before.

Would it help if individuals were to address a tiny bit of the vast problem, or did it really have to be dealt with as a whole, by a government institution such as the one our visitor represented, for example? Who was more likely to make the right decision? And was it an either-or question? Perhaps, but there again, perhaps not. Could a well-meaning gesture end up doing more harm than good, because the perpetrator hadn't realised it would have knock-on effects? Or would you not just paralyse yourself into inaction by worrying about that?

I frowned and looked down. It was too difficult to meet the children's expectant gazes. They asked for too much, wanted so much, needed so much.

One by one the children lowered their eyes. Some turned to look into the distance for a few seconds, before they resumed their play.

'*Pole sana.* Very sorry,' I muttered. But no-one was listening any more.

Another boy, Benedict, had come in, but unlike Joffre with the monkey, Benedict was reminded by the other children that he wasn't one of the chosen few. They appeared to take delight in telling him this, and he looked so dejected. I shuddered at the unfairness of it, but I was reluctant to intervene. I did not want to open the floodgates.

I watched as he walked miserably back towards the gate. His shirt ended raggedly just above his bony shoulder blades.

I couldn't stand it. 'Come back, Benedict,' I said. 'Have a banana.'

Friday Evening

As soon as Jeff came home he took a beer from the fridge and collapsed into a chair. 'How was your day, Laura?'

'I had a pile of kids in here. You know, they don't go to school because their parents can't afford the fees.'

'Yes, that's IMF policy. Everything has to be paid for.'

'But that's crazy! How can things get better if people don't get an education?'

'Better for whom? As long as it looks right on the balance sheet it's good enough for them.' Jeff took a long sip of his beer. It was hot outside. He must have had an exhausting day.

I sat down next to him. 'Anyway, I was thinking, should we pay those kids' fees?'

'What kids? There are several million out there who can't afford the fees.'

'No, I mean just the six who were here today. I know it's not much,' I shrugged. 'It's just to do what we can, I mean.'

'We could pay for a lot more than six. We could give away all our money until we're as poor as they are. Is that what you want?'

I sighed. 'You're too logical. I just want to help. Just to do one little bit. That's what you do, as the obstetrician here, isn't it?'

'No, it's not the same. You want to reverse the effects of bad policy, but it's hopeless. It's like putting sticking plasters on gushing wounds, when the victim is still being hacked to death.'

'You're probably right, but I just feel so guilty.' I got up to serve the meal.

'Pay their fees, then, if it makes you feel better,' Jeff called after me. 'But do it quietly.'

'Ok, I will. Just to alleviate my guilt, if nothing else.'

'I don't think it will.'

7

Saturday

I was annoyed to discover that Saturday was a normal working day. I had been looking forward to spending it with Jeff for a change, and perhaps even visiting a tourist attraction, like a safari park. Now I realised there would never be enough time, normally, for weekends away.

It also meant that Hope would turn up that morning. I had harboured a notion that the girl might have taken the hint and not come back after my cool words about her negligence towards Annabel.

She did turn up.

After the swimming pool incident I was not going to leave Annabel alone again with her, so the only use I had for her was help with learning Swahili.

Hope had no aptitude for this, either. If I asked her the Swahili for a word that was not in the dictionary, she would take it from me and leaf through it exasperatingly slowly until she was satisfied the word was indeed not there, then she would declare that the word did not exist.

But there had to be a word for 'shower', I would insist, or for 'toy'. But Hope would shake her head. No, there was not.

I was about to give up in despair, when Hope unexpectedly assumed an air of enthusiasm.

'When you go to England,' she said, 'I want to come with you.'

I smiled. It was easy to get out of that one. I did a quick mental calculation. 'The flight would cost a million shillings.'

'Yes?' She still looked hopeful.

I could hardly believe her naivety. No-one on a local wage could ever afford anything that cost a million shillings. Or did she expect us to pay her fare? She probably did. The cheek of it!

Then I checked myself. It was so terribly easy to get into the role of snobbish colonial white lady. Was it really so ridiculous to hope for an expenses-paid trip to England? I expected my own fare to be paid for, after all.

I felt a surge of guilt, then annoyance that Hope could do that to me. I wanted rid of her. Anyway I had a plan, which involved going out. If I dealt with the girl straightaway, I could get on with it. I fetched my purse.

'I'm going to put Annabel in kindergarten, so I won't need you any more, Hope.' I tried not to look pleased, but I suspected I did.

'But you still need me to teach you Swahili,' said Hope.

'No. I won't. You have taught me enough, now. Thank you very much. So take today's pay, and an extra four dollars.' I handed her a five-dollar bill.

Hope's eyes lit up momentarily on seeing the five dollars. Then it dawned on her that she was being sacked, and her eyes filled with tears.

I had feared this would happen. I felt horrible, but I wanted to get it over with. 'Yes, I'm sorry, but it doesn't work anymore. Now, if you'll excuse me, I need to go into town. So, thank you for everything, Hope'

I held out my hand to the girl, but she declined it, and turned and left without a word. Watching her go, I felt both guilty and relieved.

I gave Hope time to get ahead, then I fetched Annabel and we set off.

My first port of call was the house of Annabel's playmates, Keni, Salome and Miki. They were all there, sitting in their yard, with what appeared to be several other siblings.

'I would like to speak to your father, please,' I said to the oldest.

'You can't. He's dead,' he replied.

'Your mother, then.'

'She's dead, too.'

'Oh! I'm sorry. Then who is the head of the household?'

'Miki got up and called through the open doorway of the house. *'Camelia! Haka Mama Annabel.'*

A teenage girl emerged from the darkness. I had seen her before, but where?

'Yes?' she asked.

I smiled at her. 'We would like to pay the children's school fees, if we may. I think it's important that the children go to school, don't you? And if you can't afford the fees, we would like to pay for you.'

I had spoken in English and it was clear that the girl had not understood a word, but Miki did a quick translation. The girl smiled and held out her hand. 'Yes,' she said.

'But I would pay the money directly to the school,' I explained.

Miki translated, and the girl's face dropped. She'd lost interest.

I waited a few moments for further response, and when none was forthcoming, I said, 'Well?'

'Yes,' said Miki.

'Yes, what?'

'You pay.'

I approached the parents of the other children who had played with Annabel the day before. After similar exchanges, I came away having promised to pay the school fees of eight children, as far as I understood. Nonetheless, if Miki was right and the fee for each child was twenty thousand shillings, it would not break the bank.

Before going to the school, Annabel and I had to visit the nunnery. Jeff and I had talked over the idea of putting Annabel into their kindergarten, and we agreed it was worth trying, even if we weren't Catholics. It wouldn't do a four-year-old any harm, we had decided.

As soon as we arrived at the nunnery, Annabel ran into the yard where the children were playing, and within minutes, she had absorbed herself into the little congregation. In her pristine rose-patterned smock, straw hat and preppy sandals, she stood out a mile from the little black children in their rags of monochrome baked mud, but Annabel was oblivious to this.

A nun emerged from the building. With a jolt, I realised I had no idea how one was supposed to greet a nun. Was I expected to be formal? What if she was the Mother Superior? Should I have been able to tell, from the size of her crucifix, or something?

I decided not to let it worry me. 'Good morning, sister,' I said. It came out sounding Bohemian. I explained who we were, and made my request. Was there room for my daughter in their kindergarten?

The nun gave an apologetic smile, or perhaps it was a condescending one. 'Normally, we would like very much to have your child, but, you see, there is a problem: it is only three weeks before the end of term.'

'Yes,' I answered, still waiting to hear about the problem, but the nun simply smiled, demurely, again.

I was tempted to say, 'So what's the problem?' but thought the better of it.

She spoke again. 'So, you see, it is really not possible until after the school holidays. You should come back then.' She indicated that she had said all she needed to, and turned away.

It was not the response I had anticipated. The nun had not seemed exactly welcoming. Maybe, I should have been more deferential to her, sworn my commitment to the Catholic Church, for example. Or perhaps the nun could tell I was not one of them; maybe, there was some sign I should have made, a genuflection, or something?

Well, if they were going to be fussy about that, perhaps Catholicism wasn't Annabel's calling, after all. I wasn't sure I wanted her to learn the cataclysm, anyway, or whatever it was they taught.

I was back to square one, however. I tried not to let it get me down. I called out to my daughter who had, apparently, already settled in very nicely to the nunnery Kindergarten. 'We have to visit the school.'

A number of children had tagged onto us along the way, which was just as well. I would have walked right past the school if our young guides had not insisted that we had arrived at it.

It was hardly even a building, but a rectangle enclosed by mud bricks to waist height, and a corrugated iron roof supported by wooden poles. But where was the blackboard, or the desks and chairs, or indeed the floor? And where were the teachers and the pupils? Nowhere in sight.

I stood there for a few minutes wondering what to do. Then, a thin man of about fifty approached. He didn't look any different from the subsistence farmers who lived in the mud hut village, but he introduced himself as the school headmaster.

I explained why I had come. 'I would like to pay the school fees for certain children, whose families, I understand, can't afford them.'

He spoke good English. 'Yes, this is very good, but you can't pay the fees here. You will need a form to pay them into the bank. And we don't have any forms here. You would need to get one from the head office.'

I asked him for directions and he replied that it was in Kubwamji, the big city, and if I couldn't go and fetch one, I would need to write to apply for one.

'But the post – I've heard it's not reliable.'

'Yes, it's true. You would be better to go yourself, or send someone.'

Kubwamji was several hours drive away and we didn't have a car. I sighed. I was trying to do a good turn. Why did they have to make it so difficult?

He clearly understood how my despair. 'Yes. Nothing works in this country. I blame the government. We cannot run the schools because the teachers' wages don't come through. So they need to work in their *shambas* and grow vegetables, if they are to have anything to eat. Sometimes they get the children to help. Then they have a little time to give lessons. But we get nothing.'

And the teachers got the children to help build their houses, I realised, remembering the line of children walking along with bricks on their heads.

The headmaster went on, 'This shirt I am wearing – it was given to me by the children's doctor. She is a good woman. It is a very good shirt.'

He must have meant Sofia. He was wearing a ladies' blouse in a style that had been fashionable some years previously.

'It must be very difficult. I'll do what I can to pay those fees.' Turning to go home, I noticed the children who had been following us had disappeared.

8

Sunday

Bliss! Today, for the first time since we had arrived, we could spend the whole day together as a family.

'Let's go for a walk before it gets too hot,' said Jeff, getting up. The sun had just risen.

He took his binoculars, and for the first time, I took my camera, and the three of us ventured out through the *shambas* and into the forest. I had not been out quite so early before, but I realised now that this was the best time of day, not yet hot, and the sun, still climbing, afforded the world an intensity of colour and relief in shadows, before it bleached everything.

There was an aura of harmony and well-being among the villagers, who were up and about already, many in their Sunday best and on their way to church. Jeff had become quite well-known among the locals already. '*Shikamoo, Doctor Whitely*', they greeted him. The children called him '*Baba Annabel*' (father of Annabel), which he encouraged. I snapped away with my camera. Some were very happy to be photographed and would pose stiffly. Others, especially women, didn't want it.

'They think the camera is taking their soul away,' said Jeff.

As usual, we gathered an entourage of children, but once we were further from the village, they dropped back and we could appreciate the wildlife more. It was more audible than visible, with plenty of shrieks and squawks. Monkeys leapt from branch to branch above us. We strained our necks to see them.

'And parrots!' Jeff exclaimed. 'Do you see them? Annabel, look at that parrot! It's got an orange belly. I think it must be the orange-bellied parrot. Here, Laura, look through the binoculars. Isn't it wonderful here?'

I took the binoculars but I didn't want to dwell too long on the parrots, having just spotted an enormous black centipede on the ground. It must have been about five inches long. Those things were vicious biters, I had read, and if you proved to be allergic to their venom, it could give you an anaphylactic shock. I kept my eyes on the ground after that.

'Watch out, Annabel!' I warned her. 'You know you must never pick up a centipede. They bite!'

Monday

Having discovered the beauty of early morning, I decided to get up promptly and go with Annabel to the market. I wanted to see if Sofia had been right about there being plenty to buy if one went soon enough.

A large group of children were waiting at the gate again. Did they assume they could come every day now, or had they come on the off-chance? I told them we were going into town, and, like before, they all came along.

And what a lovely surprise. The market was a riot of colour and activity, sounds and smells, and good ones, unlike that first day. I took in the sight of the women moving around, big hips swaying as they set up stalls, their clothes and head-wraps a kaleidoscope of red, orange, magenta, purple, yellow. Children and goats darted around their legs, laughter and song in the air.

Sofia had indeed been right. Mountains of fruits and vegetables were piling up: fat pineapples, enormous melons, papayas, guavas, rosy red pomegranates, pale golden passion fruits, all shapes, colours and sizes of bananas, cobs of fresh corn, glistening tomatoes, peppers, okra, and spices! Cinnamon, cardamom, cloves, saffron, ginger, chillies. I took in their warm earthy colours and sharp aromas. And it was all fresh. There were lentils too, and rice, and peanuts, and all kinds of beans.

What had I been thinking about on that first morning? Certainly, there was produce I didn't recognise, things which looked like one would have to spend hours pounding, meat that looked unappetising, and fish I wasn't sure about. But they were not covered in flies like before. Perhaps those came later in the day.

Then the smell of newly-baked bread wafted towards us. I bought a huge flatbread for Annabel and me to share, and we stuffed it into our mouths there and then. But our companions, the children who had come with us, were looking on enviously. So I bought another two or three for them to share.

I set about buying food with enthusiasm. I was so excited by the thought of surprising Jeff with a delicious spicy stew, I bought far more than would go into the shopping bag. But the children negotiated extra sacks, they piled the goods into them, and took it upon themselves to carry it all for me.

Before going home, we stopped off for fizzy drinks. Unlike the food, these were not so cheap and I was reluctant to buy the hoards of children one each. But I didn't want to share our drinks either, because they were bound to have all sorts of germs I preferred them not to pass on. I bought Annabel and myself a bottle each, and three for the rest of them to share. I felt mean about it, but they didn't seem to mind.

When we got back to the house I tipped the boys who had carried the shopping, glad not to have needed to carry any of it myself, because Annabel pleaded to go on my shoulders for the last stretch. It was a long walk for her in the heat. Lackeys or none, we were still going to need a car.

I had no idea how much to tip the boys but they seemed to be overjoyed with what I gave them, even though, when I thought about it later, it was a ridiculously small amount.

The children wanted to stay to play. I let about ten of them in. I felt guilty about promising to pay all those school fees, when it seemed unlikely that I would now, not wanting to go to the city. It was a long way, I would have had to take the bus, wouldn't have known my way around, and didn't speak the language. I hadn't bargained on it being so complicated.

So I was feeling benevolent towards the children. I let them amuse themselves while I started cooking. The girls wanted to help, however, and when Mary, the housemaid, finished cleaning she came and took over. By the end of the morning, a huge pot of spicy stew was bubbling on the stove. Before they all left, it seemed only right to give them a bowlful each.

Monday Afternoon

I need not have worried about how to get those forms for paying the school fees. That afternoon, a young man, who introduced himself as Abel, the school timekeeper, came to the door and offered to go and pick up the forms for me. Word must have spread.

'Well, if you're going that way, anyway, that would be very kind of you.'

'Yes, I can do it for you.'

'Fine. That's great. Because I wouldn't have been sure where to go, and all that.'

Abel said nothing, so I added, 'That would be very helpful. I said I would pay eight children's fees, so I suppose I'll need eight forms.'

'Yes. Eight forms. The thing is, Mrs Whitelady, there is a small problem.'

'Is there?'

'Yes.' There was a pause before he spoke again. 'There is a difficulty, because I do not have the bus fare to go to the office to pick up the forms.'

'Oh! That's all right. I can give you the money for the fare. No problem. How much is it?' I got my purse.

'It is two thousand shillings. Two thousand to go, and two thousand to come back.'

'No problem. I would have had to pay that myself, if I had gone. You're saving me the bother.'

Abel took the money, but he showed no signs of leaving. I was now wondering whether to trust him.

'There is another thing,' he said eventually. 'I am the school timekeeper. I need to know the time, always, so that I can ring the bell at the start and finish of every lesson. But I don't have a watch.' He paused, for effect, presumably.

'Oh yes?' I said, but I knew what was coming.

'I could buy one when I go to Kubwamji, but they cost twenty thousand shillings. This is a problem for me.'

I sighed. It looked very much like the thin edge of a wedge. I didn't want to be foolish, but I didn't want to be mean either. 'I'll think about it,' I said. 'I mean, I'll need to ask my husband.' It was a pathetic get-out, but convenient, nonetheless.

Abel seemed to accept this. 'Yes, please ask him.'

Monday evening

Jeff had still not come home by the time it got dark, but I didn't worry so much this time as that first evening. Mondays were always busy days for doctors. They had all the ailments of the weekend to catch up on.

I had left the door to the veranda open. Now something came in. It made a loud whirring noise. At first I thought it must be some child's toy. Then I saw it. It was the most enormous insect I had ever seen. It looked formidable. I stood, wide-eyed and appalled, as I watched it fly around the room. *Oh my God! What should I do?*

It thudded into the wall and fell onto the back of the sofa. Was it dead?

I could get a good look at it now. It was a hideous black beetle; it must have been about five inches long, and it had huge fat mandibles. I shuddered. *Please be dead now!*

I was afraid to touch it in case it wasn't. I decided to watch it for a few more minutes, to make sure it could do no more harm, before scooping it up and chucking it out.

But then it moved. First it waved its antennae about, then those awful pincers. What could it do to us? *Jeff, please come home.* I needed to catch it, but how. The only container big enough was a saucepan. I went to fetch one.

'Annabel, don't touch it, will you? Come with me.' I could not turn my back on it while in the same room.

It was still there when we got back, twitching its wings. I wasted no time, and slammed the saucepan on top of it, then pressed the rim into the curve of the sofa, lest it should get through the gap. But what to do now? I was terrified it would squeeze its way out.

'Annabel, please fetch a saucepan lid.'

'Where?'

'You know where. In the kitchen,' I said, trying but failing to keep my voice calm.

She ran through, and after an agonising minute of clattering she came back with one. But it was the wrong size. It would be worse than nothing at all.

'Please find one the right size, Annabel.'

'This one will do,' she said, plaintively.

Ideally, I would not have displayed to her how terrified I was, but it was hopeless. 'No, it will not do! Please, Annabel!' *Please, Jeff, please come home!*

Finally, Annabel produced the fitting lid. As I slid it between the saucepan and the sofa there was a loud hissing noise from inside, which startled me so much I almost dropped everything. But I managed. Then I had to turn it round. I prayed to God it would not escape. It didn't, but it thudded around the saucepan, vigorously. Now I couldn't leave it or it would push the lid off and take its revenge. I could not release it outside either, in case it attacked, or came back into the house before I could shut the door. So with my outstretched hand pressing firmly on the lid, I sat there until Jeff came home.

'Hello! Sorry I'm late,' he called cheerily. 'Ooh, have you cooked something nice? Let's have a look.'

'No!' I shrieked as he tried to lift the lid of the saucepan on my lap. 'Oh, Jeff! It's the most awful insect! I have never seen anything like it!'

Jeff prised the pan out of my hands and took it outside. Ignoring my warnings, he lifted the lid cautiously, and looked inside. The insect lay still.

'Wow!' said Jeff. 'It's a rhino beetle!'

'Are they dangerous? What will it do?'

'Nothing. They're harmless. Look, they hiss if you poke them.' He pressed his finger on its back and like before, it gave out the most awful hiss.

'Do you want to have a go, Annabel?' he asked.

Annabel, who was peering out from behind my legs, shook her head.

'Please get rid of that disgusting creature,' I pleaded.

Jeff took the rhino beetle outside and let it fly off. He came back grinning. 'But you have cooked something nice, haven't you? I can smell it.'

I felt peeved. I wasn't sure whether I was more annoyed with myself for being afraid, pointlessly, or with Jeff, for giving me no condolence. Anyway, Annabel lifted me out of it.

'Daddy, we went to the market and bought lots of vegetables and we all cooked them and we all ate them and we nearly didn't leave any left for you. We nearly forgot about you.'

'But we didn't, did we, Annabel? Of course, there's some left for you.'

'That's nice. So, who all was that? Did you have lots of friends here today again?'

I gave him a quick run-down on our day, finishing with an account of Abel, the school timekeeper, and his request for a watch.

Jeff laughed. 'I think you should get him a wind-up clock.'

9

Tuesday.

Annabel was having an afternoon siesta and I was sitting on our front porch reading when Philippe came past. He had a towel round his waist, having just come from the swimming pool.

'It's very hot today, isn't it?' If there was ever a banal comment, that was it. It was always very hot here. I wondered why he was not at work.

'Yes, it is too hot. It makes one very tired.' Philippe made no move to go.

'I'm so glad I don't have to work when it's like this,' I continued, by way of conversation. 'It must be unbearable at the hospital.'

'Yes, it is so.' Then, 'Would you like to come for a drink?'

Philippe always seemed so sad. He was probably very lonely. He needed friends and so did I. His house was only next door. If Annabel woke up I would hear her. 'Why not? Yes, I'd like to.'

His house, unlike ours, was cool, clean and orderly. Two white sofas faced a glass-topped coffee table, and a glass and aluminium bookcase covered one wall. A few sculptures with sensuous curves, probably carved from ivory, punctuated the rest of the space.

'Please.' He gestured for me to sit down. 'What will you drink? You English people like gin and tonic, don't you?'

'Oh just a soft drink for me, please. Water is fine. I never drink alcohol before sunset. Or just a tonic. That's fine.'

Philippe had already opened a bottle of tonic and laden two glasses with ice and lemon. 'Please join me.' He was pouring the gin.

He handed me a glass, then paused. 'Do you mind if I remain undressed?'

'No, not at all, when it's so hot. Cheers.' I took a sip of my drink, then laid it on the coffee table. When I glanced up again, Philippe had moved slightly further away, and he had let his towel slip off. If he had had swimming shorts on, he had let those slip off too. He was standing, looking at me.

His body was a sorry specimen of the male physique. Little ripples of flesh, devoid of muscle, hung off his aging frame. I looked away again quickly, picked up my drink, and rose to browse his books. He had a lot about art, especially sculpture. I pulled one out. It had a photograph of Michelangelo's David on the cover.

'Oh, I love Michelangelo,' I said, then realising the contrast between David and Philippe, hurriedly put it back. I scanned the shelves. 'Have you visited many art galleries?'

'Of course.' His voice was terse, now; it came from further away. I looked round to see him getting dressed hastily.

What to do? I searched for a suitable book – 'Women in Art' – 'The Naked Body' – 'The Female Form' – 'The Drawings of Leonardo da Vinci'. I pulled that one out. I sat down with it, murmuring an occasional comment of appraisal, as I thumbed through it and sipped my drink. Philippe did not come to sit down. He seemed to be occupied at the drinks cabinet.

I got up. 'I think I heard Annabel,' I lied. 'I'd better go. Thank you so much for the drink.'

'It's nothing,' he said. He sounded miserable. As I turned to say goodbye, he said, 'Laura, you won't say anything to anyone, will you?'

'Of course not,' I smiled, and made my exit.

Tuesday Evening.

'Hello, Laura, my love. Hello Annabel. How was your day?'

'Hi! Fine.' I gave Jeff a peck on the cheek. 'How was yours?'

'Not bad – pretty good, actually.' He sounded surprised. 'No one died today.'

'Amazing! It can't get much better than that, can it?'

Jeff laughed. 'And what did you do today, Annabel?'

Annabel didn't answer, so I did. 'We got up early again, didn't we? To go to the market, but first Abel turned up. I told him you wouldn't pay for a watch. But he seemed to take it in good grace. I gave him money for the bus fares so he could pick up the forms.'

'So he got a free trip to town. Good.'

We were both quiet for a few minutes. I wondered if Jeff could read my face, that I was keeping something from him. Or would he smell the gin on my breath?

Eventually, I said, 'Philippe invited me in for a drink, this afternoon.'

'That's nice. So you're making friends. How was it?'

What to tell him? My eyes slid to the side of the room that was taken up by Annabel's playthings. 'His house is very orderly. No clutter at all. Just a few sculptures, abstract female figures, I suppose they were, with sensual curves.'

Jeff chuckled. 'He's probably sex-starved.'

'Well, I get the feeling he's very lonely, anyway.'

'I get the feeling he's lost the plot, at work. He probably ought to retire.'

'He'd probably like to,' I said, and got up to see to the dinner. That was enough about Philippe.

Wednesday

Abel turned up first thing next morning, having fulfilled his promise to pick up the school fee forms.

I thanked him.

'Mrs Whitelady,' he said. 'I would like to invite you to our village. My brother is having his confirmation tomorrow. It is a very special occasion.' He assured me that it would not be far to walk, so I agreed.

'And will you bring your camera? We would like you to take photographs.'

'All right,' I said, although I had no way of getting film developed apart from getting someone to take it back to Europe and waiting for their return.

The children had turned up. This time there were rather more than ten of them, which was not surprising. Not only would they get to play with Annabel's toys, but now they would be hoping for a bowlful of vegetable stew, as they'd had on the previous two days.

We had finished off the first lot far sooner than I had expected. I felt I had bought enough to last a week but I hadn't bargained on feeding a multitude. I was saved from another trek to the market, however, because someone came to our door, peddling vegetables. There was not much choice, and I was sure he was charging over the odds for them, but it did save me the trek.

It also meant I could get on with learning Swahili. I got out my books: a dictionary, a grammar book and a phrasebook.

Annabel's friends were absorbed in play, so I felt uninhibited about reading aloud from the phrasebook.

'Hii ndiyo njia ya kwenda sokoni?'
'Hii ndiyo njia ya kwenda benki?'

The children looked up and stared at me in bafflement.

Of course, my questions were nonsensical. Was this the way to the market place, the bank? I explained. '*Mimi ni kujifunza kiswahili*'.

Their faces cleared. They understood. I was trying to learn their language. Then it dawned on me. They could help me.

'*Ni kitu gani?*' I said, holding up the book. 'What is this?'

'*Kitabu*', Micki answered.

'*Ni kitu gani?*' I held up my pen.

'*Kalamu.*' Several of them answered this time.

I needed to write these words down. I picked up my notebook. '*Kalamu.* How you do spell it?' I didn't know how to ask that in Swahili, so I indicated that they should write it.

Micki picked up the pen and fumbled with it. It seemed he hadn't used one for a long time. With hesitation, he started writing down the word, but two of the other children were telling him he was getting it wrong. One of them grabbed the pen and started writing, but he wasn't sure either.

These children could hardly write.

That gave me another idea. They could teach me Swahili, and I could give them writing practice. I went to fetch paper and pens for all of them. I picked up Annabel's magnetic letter set, too. She could also benefit from this. The children could help her, and help themselves at the same time.

Thursday.

I had to take those school-fee forms to the bank. We had all been pleased with our morning of *Shule* the day before, and I didn't want to break the momentum, but real school was more important for the children. So, before the sun got too hot, I walked with my entourage into town.

Unlike the first time at the bank, when Edward had arranged things for me, I had no alternative but to take my place in the queue. Thankfully, I was able to sit down, but the wait was tedious, especially for Annabel. The other children had not been allowed in. I now realised that every visit to the bank was going to take up a whole morning, and this meant every time I needed cash, because there were no automatic cash dispensers.

At last my turn came. Here, at least, I knew I could speak English.

'Good morning. I would like to pay these children's school fees from our account.'

The bank clerk gave the forms a prolonged stare, shuffling from one to the other.

'So, Mrs Whitely,' he said at last. 'You would like to pay these school fees, from your own account. But these are not your children. I think this will be a problem. I must ask my supervisor.'

He disappeared for several minutes. I wished I could have asked Edward to negotiate this for me, but I feared I was not in his good books after having sacked his daughter. We had passed each other on the path the day before, and his greeting seemed less than warm.

The bank clerk came back. 'Yes, it is possible for you to pay the school fees. We can arrange this.'

Protracted form-filling ensued.

Finally, he said, 'Now, it is necessary for you to sign here. – Thank you. - Now, God willing, the documentation will completed for the beginning of next term.'

'Next term? I was hoping the children could go to school with their receipts tomorrow.'

'No, Mrs Whitely, unfortunately, that is not possible. The children must wait until the notification from the education department comes through that the fees are paid.'

'And how long will that take?'

'Perhaps before the beginning of next term. We can only hope. It is up to the Good Lord. He will surely acknowledge your good deed, Mrs Whitely.'

'Listen, why don't you just give me the receipts and I'll give them to the children to show the school that their fees have been paid?'

'I don't think you understand, Mrs Whitely. That is not possible. We must follow the correct procedure.'

I gave up. I had done what I could.

Thursday afternoon.

Abel turned up promptly to take me to his village, as we had arranged. Annabel had to come, too, and our usual companions would have followed, but Abel had sharp words with them and they stayed behind.

I was relieved that he was true to his word about it not being very far. It was a cluster of mud huts right behind the school.

His brother's confirmation was obviously a big deal, or perhaps it was my coming that was the big event, because as soon as we arrived, about twenty women, dressed in vivid *kangas* and turbans, started dancing and singing. The show was clearly for my benefit. What exactly had Abel told them about me – that I was some kind of VIP? I took several photos, as was expected, knowing, guiltily, that it would be an eternity before they saw them.

'Where's your brother?' I asked Abel.

'He is in his house. He must not come out yet.'

It was hot. Sweat poured from my brow. I made to remove my sunhat, but Abel stopped me. 'Please, Mrs Whitelady, would you keep your hat on?'

I complied, smiling. 'If it's important to you.'

Abel showed me round his village and introduced me to his family. They invited me to participate in the meal. It didn't look at all appetising; it was some kind of porridge. But, here, it was extremely rude to refuse to take part in a meal when offered, so I scooped up a token bit and urged Annabel to do the same. It was as tasteless as it looked.

On leaving, they presented me with eggs. This was nice; we hadn't had eggs since we had come to Africa. I did wonder whether I could get them home without breaking them. I also wondered how much my acceptance of this gift was indebting me to them.

Abel took me to the school, which I had seen already. It seemed to me that it needed an awful lot, like desks, chairs, walls, a blackboard, a floor, before it needed a watch for its timekeeper. I tried to find a delicate way of suggesting this.

Abel must have read my mind. 'Our school needs many things but the most important thing is to be able to keep time, and that is why I need a watch.'

'Wouldn't a big clock, that everyone could see, be better? One that you could wind up, so that you wouldn't have to worry about batteries or power cuts?'

For a moment Abel looked slightly disturbed by this suggestion. Then he shook his head. No, he told me. That was not appropriate. Only a watch that he could wear would be appropriate.

I didn't argue with him. I wanted to get back. 'I'll see what I can do,' I said, feebly.

When we got back to the compound, Camelia, the teenage sister of Miki, Salome and Keni, whose house we had gone to on Saturday, emerged from Philippe's bungalow. He stood in the doorway, naked except for a towel round his waist. I knew I had seen the girl somewhere before. Now I remembered. She had been the prostitute at the bar in town. It made sense. She was the head of a family of orphans, and this was how she fed them.

Thursday evening.

Once Annabel was in bed, I couldn't hold from Jeff what I had seen.
'It's really quite disturbing. I mean, he's a gynaecologist!'
I realised my voice was betraying undue emotion. I had lost sympathy with Philippe, having seen that my encounter with him was not an isolated incident, but a custom.
'Well, I'm sure he uses condoms,' said Jeff.
'I don't care. It's not right!'

10

Friday

Today I was to get another lesson about queues, this time at the hospital, so I should have known better, but I panicked.

Annabel was playing with her friends, as usual. The morning had gone well. We'd had another reciprocal Swahili and writing lesson, and I had added in some instruction about geometry while we were chopping the vegetables. I should not have been surprised that many of them already knew how to cut shapes. They showed no lack of creativity and ingenuity in the way they rearranged them. They just lacked formal instruction.

Once the stew was cooking, we continued in the same vein, with a lesson about capacity disguised as a tea party. They enjoyed this; it was obviously a novel experience. They got engrossed in their game of pretend, and as I could hardly make out a word of their chatter, I left them to it and got on with some Swahili learning.

An outburst of laughter made me look up. Annabel was the centre of attention. She, like all the other children, was covered in mud. To supplement the water for their tea party, they had brought soil from the garden onto the veranda, and had made mud tea.

In England I would not have bothered about this. But in here Africa, there were so many pathogens in the soil. I was appalled. Annabel had forgotten to pretend, and she had gulped down a whole cupful of the African dirt. She stuck her tongue out in disgust, but like the other children she found it funny. I, on the other hand, did not.

Oh my God! I pulled her over to the sink and rinsed out her mouth. But there was no saying what dreadful, possibly fatal things she had already swallowed. It was going to require more drastic action.

I grabbed her arm. 'Come on, darling, we're going to go down to the hospital to get you cleaned up.' I spared her the details that ran through my head.

I took her to paediatrics. Perhaps I subconsciously assumed we should get preferential treatment, but I was hardly aware of the great long queue of mothers with sick children waiting to see Sofia. I dashed past them and straight into her 'surgery', which was really just a sectioned-off part of the corridor.

'Oh Sofia, I don't know what to do! Annabel has just swallowed a whole cupful of soil from the garden. Do we need to make her sick? Should we pump her stomach?'

Sofia was infuriatingly calm. 'Don't worry,' she said. 'At worst, she will get a few parasites; then we can de-worm her.'

This made me squirm. I had read all about these intestinal parasites so common in Sub-Saharan Africa.

For a start, there were hookworms in the ground, which usually got into the blood system through bare feet. They went through the heart and into the lungs from where they would be coughed up and swallowed. Once inside the intestines, they sucked voraciously, damaged the mucous membranes and gave the host anaemia, causing intellectual, cognitive and growth retardation.

Even more disturbing was the giant intestinal roundworm, the most common worm infection. One could ingest huge numbers of the eggs, which, once hatched, could grow up to fourteen inches long inside the intestine. They caused morbidity by depleting the host of nutrition, affecting cognitive processes, and inducing tissue reactions and verminous intoxication. They could obstruct the intestine or cause rectal prolapse. They got into the lungs where they caused haemorrhage, inflammation, bacterial infection and allergy. They could even be fatal.

But it got worse. There was the tapeworm. It actually attached itself to the intestinal wall with sucking hooks and could grow up to thirty metres long. Ingesting eggs straight from the ground could make one an intermediate host, in which case they would invade muscle tissue and cause even more damage. They could also obstruct the intestine, and larvae could even migrate to the brain and cause neurological problems. This could take years to develop before symptoms appeared.

There were also whipworms and pinworms, perhaps not quite so awful, but still most unwelcome.

I knew all about these parasites because I had an appalled fascination for them. The thought that one, or probably several, of those worms were going to grow inside my little girl filled me with disgust.

But what could I do? The doctor had spoken. It wasn't an emergency. Indeed, when I turned to go, I saw the long queue of anxious mothers with sick and wailing children, presumably, all with more urgent problems. Then I realised that the next time we needed medical attention, we really ought to wait our turn.

'Sorry for barging in on you,' I said to Sofia. 'I suppose I just panicked.'

'Don't worry,' she said. She opened a plastic box. 'Annabel, I have something for you.' She pulled out a pineapple cube with a cocktail stick and gave it to her. 'Mmmm'.

As we made to go Sofia called me back. 'Oh, Laura, did you ever give any more thought to the secretary job? I do need someone to sort out my records.'

I looked around. There were no records visible. 'Well – what system do you use?' I asked, playing for time.

Sofia picked up a school exercise book. 'This is it. It is completely inadequate, I know, but what can I do? I really need a computer, but there is no money. I write down everything in here, but it's hopeless. I can't find anything or anybody again. I need someone to help me.'

I had to tell her again that I wasn't free to work, but I felt mean. 'Perhaps I could look at your records sometime and help you work out a system.'

Sofia brought out a handful of exercise books from her desk drawer. 'Here, you can take these now. I never look at them. If you can devise a system that works without a computer, I will be very surprised, but I will be very grateful.'

'I'll take a look at them this evening,' I said.

'Oh, but Laura,' Sofia called as I turned to go. 'You do realise there's no money to pay you, don't you?'

'Of course,' I replied.'

Friday evening

I shook my head in amazement when I browsed through the paediatric records. Under each date, all she had scribbled in was a child's first name, a few symptoms, her diagnosis, and treatment. But how many *Mohammeds* were there, or *Erics*? There was no apparent connection between visits, so how did she retrieve a patient's history? And if she didn't, what was the point of keeping records? I put this to Jeff.

'We have to keep records. But Sofia's right. It's pretty impossible without a computer, and it would need some pretty slick software.'

'Hospitals have kept patients' records for eons without computers. What's wrong with a card index system? I'm really surprised at Sofia. She seems so organised and efficient.'

'Sofia likes to give the impression of being ultra-efficient, but she rides over things too much. Look at how she's treated Annabel, for instance.'

'Yes, I think it's appalling! Jeff, what are we going to do?'

Jeff shifted in his chair. 'She probably did the right thing in the circumstances. Annabel's not ill yet. Sofia has more important things to attend to.'

I gaped at his shift in loyalties. What kind of relationship did he have with Sofia? 'Anyway, surely it's important to keep medical records. These notes here are downright sloppy. She hasn't even put in the patient's surname.'

'No, she only goes through the motions of keeping records because she knows it's hopeless. The surname's not reliable. It can change. The mothers don't really know what you mean by a surname. It's not the same here as in Europe.'

'You can tell me that again.'

'The parents die and the children have to be adopted. Even the first name can change. And there's no fixed spelling. It's the same with their address – no house number, no street name, nobody knows how to spell the village name – they move around anyway. And date of birth's no good either – the mother doesn't usually know it.'

'She should give every patient a number, then.'

'They'd forget it. You can't expect them to bring an ID card either.'

'You could stamp the number on them.'

'What, with a branding iron?'

And so it went on. I wanted to demonstrate that a workable system was possible. I thought I had found a crack in Sofia's impeccability. Now Jeff was telling me her poor record-keeping was not sloppiness but pragmatism. I wanted to get one up on them both.

I would design a system for her. We agreed to meet that Sunday to discuss it.

'I'll come too, then,' said Jeff. 'I need to get a system worked out, too.'

11

Saturday

Livingstone and Jared, the two junior doctors who lived on our compound, were going on leave the next day, and they offered to take any letters to Kubwamji from where they could be sent on.

The nearest thing we had to a reliable postal service in Wenduzu was to give one's letters to a trustworthy person who happened to be going to the city. They would drop them off at the health department headquarters from where, hopefully, they would be picked up by the postal service. We relied upon a similar arrangement for incoming letters, although not for parcels. Urgent messages could be telexed straight to the hospital.

Entrusted people did not travel to the city very often, so both Jeff and I took this chance to write to our families.

What would I say? I should have had plenty to write about, but faced with a blank page, I found it not so easy. It wasn't that I didn't want to write home. I was acutely homesick. But I was wary of letting too much emotion flood onto the page. How could I distil all the experiences of the last two weeks, including quite a few traumas, into a presentable account of a few paragraphs? Eventually I wrote:

Dear Mum and Dad,

Greetings from Africa! I hope this finds you good and well, and that this letter does not take very long to arrive.

We have been here two weeks now. We arrived safely and we have settled into our new home in the staff housing compound. We have a bungalow in a courtyard surrounded by a high wall, with a security guard, so we feel very safe. We also have a swimming pool here, which is a godsend, because it gets very hot. We also have a housemaid!

Jeff has settled down well at work. He is very happy, if somewhat overwhelmed. The work is much harder here, but he knew it would be.

Annabel is fine too. She has lots of friends who come to the house everyday and she is learning to swim.

I am fine too. For the first week I had a girl to teach me Swahili, and look after Annabel. I have taken on some work – sorting out the paediatrician's records. We have been to a couple of parties at her place. She is the most amazing cook.

I was also invited to the confirmation of someone's brother, where I took a lot of photos. Would you mind getting the enclosed spool developed and sending the photos back when you get a chance? There's no photo service anywhere near here. Please just keep the photos of Annabel. And could you send duplicates to Jeff's parents, please?

Wenduzu is a very pleasant and peaceful place and everyone is very friendly. There's not much to the town, but it has a market. The fruit and veg are incredibly cheap! Banana trees are everywhere. There's lots of interesting wildlife, too. Last Sunday we went for a walk in the rainforest and saw monkeys and parrots.

I miss you very much. Please do write when you can and tell me all about everything that's going on. I believe the address in London we gave you still works.

Love and hugs to you both from me, Jeff and Annabel.

I felt I should have written much more, considering the rarity of opportunity to send a letter. But there was so much I couldn't tell them.

So I didn't mention how lonely and out out-of-place I felt, or how I had failed to find a role for myself, or that although I had taken on some sorting out of records, I was full of misgivings about it.

I declined to mention that the girl I had hired was the administrator's daughter and I had sacked her because she could have let Annabel drown in the swimming pool. I certainly didn't tell them that their granddaughter had swallowed a load of dirt and that she was probably harbouring parasitic worms, nor that the 'interesting wildlife' mainly consisted of the most horrendous creepy crawlies and that they were everywhere.

I didn't tell them that although food was very cheap, I was buying vast amounts of it to feed hoards of children because they seemed so undernourished. I omitted the fact that several of Annabel's friends were AIDS orphans, and that their oldest sister provided for them by selling sex, and that one of her customers was the hospital gynaecologist. I certainly didn't mention that we suspected Mary, our housemaid, also had AIDS, because her baby had died. I hadn't even mentioned that Annabel's friends were black.

I left out how harrowing Jeff's job was because there were so many stillbirths and even women dying in childbirth, and that the hospital was vastly under-resourced, nor that all sorts of everyday things were not available, and that nothing could be taken for granted, electricity, for example.

Nor did I mention that that I had paid eight children's school fees, and shelled out quite a lot of money besides, on other people asking for this and that, and that if we weren't careful there wouldn't be enough to last the month. I did not explain that I felt permanently awkward and guilty, because the economic gap between us and them was so vast.

My parents would not have understood.

Livingstone and Jared invited me into their house, even though they were busy packing. They looked excited. They were going back to their home town to visit family, they told me.

'Are you brothers?' I asked them. They were good-looking young men, shy, but always polite, and presumably hard-working. I didn't see them very often.

They looked at each other and smiled. 'No, we're not brothers,' said Livingstone.

'We're just good friends,' said Jared.

I had thought as much. They lived together, worked together, went on holiday together. I suspected they were more than good friends, but I didn't want to know. I had heard that in many African countries homosexuality was not tolerated and was often treated very harshly indeed. It might even have been the case that one was breaking the law by failing to report a person one suspected was gay. I silently wished them discretion.

'Have a good holiday,' I said, before leaving. 'I'm really grateful to you for taking our letters,' I added, meaning it. There was no saying how long our letters would take to get there, nor when we might receive replies, if at all, but, at last, we could send our parents the message that we were all right.

12

Sunday

Of course, Annabel had to come to Sofia and Roy's too. We took along toys for her but she didn't need them, as I was reminded as soon as we entered their house, that they had four children. Sofia led Annabel by the hand to their playroom where her eyes filled with delight.

It was full of the most fabulous playthings, far more wonderful than the ones we had brought with us. There were dolls everywhere, teddies, soft toys of every species, stacks of games and construction sets. But even more amazing were the large items: a dolls' house, a dolls' pram. My eyes gaped around the room. A Wendy house, a rocking-horse, a train-set. And a piano, for goodness sake!

'Wow!' I gasped. 'But how did you manage to bring all these things here?'

'The piano, we had flown in,' said Sofia, laughing. 'But the toys, they have accumulated over the years. Remember we have been here quite a long time.'

My amazement was tinged a little, with the sobering thought that just outside were hundreds of children with hardly a lego-brick between them.

'Now, first of all, Annabel, what would you like to drink?' asked Sofia. ' We have pineapple juice, mango juice, lemon or passion-fruit cocktail?'

Our daughter was mesmerised. It was such a long time since she'd had anything other than *Agent Orange*.

'I think you'd like pineapple best,' I said.

'I would love some passion-fruit cocktail,' Jeff said.

I resisted the temptation to glare at him for the innuendo, and accepted some too. 'But where on Earth do you get hold of all this here?'

85

'The juice? I make my own,' said Sofia. Don't you have a juicer? You can borrow mine, if you like.'

'Let's go into the summerhouse,' she said after pouring us all drinks. 'It's cooler there and Annabel can play in the garden.' She led us down the garden path. My face brushed against some zebra-patterned silk sheets that were hanging up to dry. They were beautifully soft and sensuous. What I would have done for sheets like those!
 Their summerhouse was an octagonal structure of wood and rattan with elaborately-styled arches, open to any breeze.
For Annabel, the garden was no less delightful. Someone had built a tree-house and attached a climbing-frame with swings and a slide.
We sat down to work out a patients' records system. Roy joined us because he said none of the doctors kept good records. I had not taken to Roy. He had come over as angry, almost bullying, to the International Development man at their dinner party. But having an overview of the hospital, he made a valuable contribution to the discussion. It occurred to me that his apparent hostility towards the VIP was more a manifestation of worry and exasperation than sheer belligerence.

By the end of the afternoon, we had agreed upon a system based on households. Village names were reliable as key bits of information. The head of each household might not be permanent but at least the patients would remember this much. The doctor would have to spend a minute or two getting enough information to home in on the right patient record, but it would be worth it. It would improve treatment, save money and probably even lives. Of course, it was far from the perfect solution. A computer system would have been much better, but that was not an option.

I left with my work cut out for several evenings. I would have to set up skeleton records to minimise the work the doctor had to do, then I had to go through Sofia's old notebooks and salvage what information I could from them, and put it into the new system. It was worrying. The method was not foolproof, and wrong information was worse than none at all. But I was glad of the activity. At last I could be useful, and it gave me something to do in the evenings after Annabel was in bed. While she was awake, work was impossible.

It would take my mind off those ubiquitous insects, which were especially bad after dark. Cockroaches had the biggest ugh factor. They were not as dreadful as rhino beetles but they were everywhere and they were disgusting. No matter how much Mary and I kept getting rid of them they always came back. One afternoon, while resting on the sofa, I watched a cockroach crawl across the ceiling above me, and it had dropped right onto my face. It was as if it had done it for spite. That wasn't even the worst, though. Annabel actually got one in her mouth. It had been in her glass of milk. I couldn't think how it got in. We got our milk straight from the cow. It was delivered to our door in a lidded urn. We had to boil it, then it went straight into the fridge. I had always felt things in the fridge were safe. Now I was reminded they were not.

At least the cockroaches didn't bite, unlike the mosquitoes. They were at their worst at dusk, although, thankfully, the malaria-carrying kind only bit between two and four in the morning, when we were safe under our nets. Ants were also everywhere. They literally came out of the woodwork, and I never stopped being amazed at their ability to get into things. For example, those little juice cartons, with the tiny aluminium seal you punched a hole in for the straw, looked intruder-proof, but ants would climb up the side of the carton, along the top, up the outside of the straw and down the inside.

I did get some satisfaction from watching them march up the walls and straight into electrical sockets. I harboured hopes that they would all get electrocuted. Certainly, they never seemed to come out from there. Were their bodies piling up inside? What were they doing to the electrical circuits?

We did get frequent power-cuts, two or three a week, their durations unpredictable, but they affected the whole area. Then there was nothing much we could do except by candlelight. That's when Jeff would pick up his guitar. It was one of the few non-essentials we had brought with us. He was a competent player. I liked it best when he played ballads. His voice was not exactly concert-standard, but it was soft and romantic. It's what made me fall in love with him, I suppose. It certainly made those times of darkness more tolerable.

Monday

After our afternoon swim and siesta, Annabel amused herself quietly with a game, so I took the opportunity to get on with my new job. The work was a lot more challenging than I had thought. I had feared at first that it would simply be drudgery. Now I realised that it would take careful planning. Moreover, I had to decipher Sofia's handwriting.

After some time, I noticed that Annabel was singing to herself, and it was a song I didn't know.

> *How many day*
> *in da week i da*
> *how many day*
> *in da week i da*
> *mande toode wende ....*

Who had taught her that? Not me. I couldn't think of anyone she had been with who spoke English.

I asked her. 'That's a nice song. Where did you learn that?'

Annabel just shrugged, and I got on with my work.

There was a knock at the door. *Hodi.* It was Mary. Had she forgotten something?

Umefika katika nyumba, she said.

'What?' I said, unsure of what she meant.

She repeated herself.

'You want me to come to your house?'

Mary nodded. She understood a little English, even if she was reluctant to speak any. She was smiling, so I trusted it was not an emergency. Even so, she had been smiling when she had told me that her baby had just died, so I couldn't be sure.

So it was with trepidation that I summoned Annabel and followed her.

Mary lived in one of the mud huts in the village. She beckoned us inside. It was dark, having no windows or other source of light apart from the way we came in. When my eyes adjusted, I noticed an elderly couple sitting on the ground. Mary introduced them to me. They were her husband's parents. Then she took me over to the other side of the hut where a man lay in a bed, her husband. We shook hands. He was very thin and obviously weak.

I reckoned I was right in guessing that Mary's baby had died of congenital AIDS. No-one really knew how many people had AIDS here. No-one liked to talk about it. There was probably an awful lot more of it than the official records estimated.

Mary gestured that we should sit down. The only seating available was a straw mat, so we settled ourselves on that and I was surprised to find it comfortable. Likewise, the mud hut was unexpectedly cool inside. Nonetheless, I would not have chosen to stay in a house like that, not in a million years. We were offered water, which we accepted. I waited to hear what she or her family had to tell, me, but it seemed there was nothing. Her husband and his parents had simply wanted to meet us.

Were there other family members who lived with them, I asked, in my patchy Swahili.

No, there were not. Mary's husband had other siblings but they had their own houses, I gathered.

So Mary had no other children?

Yes, three, she indicated.

So where were they?

They had died, she told me, quietly but calmly.

Like before, I was surprised at the apparent lack of emotion. Was that because displays of grief were frowned upon, or because death was such a common ocurrence that no-one got upset, or because one could quite easily become

overwhelemed by so many tragedies, one if one succumbed? Or was it because AIDS was so shameful that one could hardly even think about it, never mind talk about it? I felt terribly sad for Mary, for all of them.
'Pole sana,' I said. I'm so sorry.

There was a silence after that. A chill came over me with a new realisation. This meant that Mary herself almost certainly had HIV even if symptoms had not yet presented themselves. I wondered how long it would take until they did. Her husband would probably die before she did. What would become of their elderly parents then? Perhaps it was just as well they had no children, although that itself must have been a great sadness and affliction.

Once again, I felt overwhelmed by the seemingly never-ending stream of woes that burdened this whole continent.

Mary took Annabel by the hand and led her outside. I followed. I took the opportunity first to say goodbye to the rest of her family. I didn't want to have to go back in again. Outside, Mary was showing Annabel some newly-born chickens. They had picked some up and were stroking them gently. Even amidst so much hopelessness, life could spring anew.

13

Tuesday

Jeff was quiet and glum when he came home from work. I suspected what was wrong. We had been there before, many times already. 'Another stillbirth?'

He nodded. 'It was a fistula problem. They come in too late for us to help them. Then afterwards it's not an emergency and we don't have the capacity to help them. And these women are rejected by their husbands and ostracized from their communities.

I shook my head in despair. 'Through ignorance, probably.'

Jeff nodded. 'And because the woman stinks of urine. And it's all for want of a simple operation. They're told they can get it fixed in the big hospital but of course they can't afford the bus fare. So it's a life sentence.'

I sighed. I felt helpless. It was a permanent feeling of being hopelessly dragged down by so much neediness all around us.

Jeff was more resilient. His pragmatic approach made sense: you do what you can and you stop worrying about what you can't. I needed to be more like him or I wouldn't survive here. That this whole continent could hardly breathe under its great burden of problems was hardly our fault, after all. There may have been a collective guilt about what we as the rich world had done, and were still doing to the third world, but it was not personal. If we had not been here to actually see all the hardship, we, like everyone else in the world, would not have been worrying about them, even though the problems would still have existed. I felt that they would go on existing, however much worrying anyone did. I hated the thought getting hard and callous, but felt I could succumb to the temptation.

'I don't know, Jeff. It seems to me that the people here make their own problems. For example, if you have ten kids, anywhere in the world you're going to be struggling. Why do they keep on having such big families? You'd think they would learn.' It was a non-sequitur to the fistula problem, but the problems of the world usually were blamed on overpopulation. It was the obvious thing.

Jeff raised his eyebrow. 'I'm surprised at you talking like that, Laura. You're the one who's always going on about the demographic transition.'

He was right. I had learned about the so-called demographic transition at university, the theory that birth rates followed death rates, going down when a country developed, for reasons like access to contraception, less reliance on child labour, and empowerment of women. It had happened in nineteenth-century Europe, and more recently in less rich countries. But until then, each child was more of an asset than a liability to their parents, because they were put to work early in life, and the children were their insurance in old age. So people had as many children as they could, the main limiting factor being the food available. So they were always on the brink of starvation.

Except, here it was in the present tense. In most of Sub-Saharan Africa they hadn't got as far as the transition.

Back home, it had always annoyed me when people put the world's problems down to over-population: that it was all those African and Asians having far too many children that were to blame for everything. It had always seemed such a cop-out from the rich world taking any responsibility itself. I would point out that the average American took thirty times as much out of the environment as the average African.

But now, seeing how close to the edge of survival the people here lived, it looked clear that they were only exacerbating their problems by having big families, and sometimes I felt those blame-shifters back home had a point.

'I know, Jeff, but you'd think they might just see what was happening in their own families. I mean, it is the nineteen-nineties. You'd think they'd be able to cotton on that if they each have ten kids, and each of them has ten kids, things are going to get a lot worse for them, not better.'

'The parents must know better than anybody what it means to have another mouth to feed. But I doubt you could persuade them with that argument. The issues must look different at family level, from the bigger scale of things, don't you think?'

I sighed. 'Maybe, but I wish they would just look ahead. I wish the damned democratic transition would hurry up. Or they wouldn't bother waiting for it, because as far as I can see, it's not going to happen. Not here.'

'Never mind. Anyway, what did you and Annabel do today?'

I hated this *don't-you-worry-your-little-head* response of Jeff's. I knew he didn't really mean to belittle me, that it only meant he was tired of talking about the subject, but I tended to get worked up about things, and I didn't like to have the discussion wound up in what seemed like a put-down manner, especially when I hadn't spoken to another adult all day.

'What do you think I've done today? I've done what I always do. I had about forty kids round here to play with Annabel's toys.'

Of course, I regretted saying this immediately, considering what kind of day Jeff had had.

'Oh Laura, I think it's great that you have all those kids round here. I'm sure they appreciate it. I'm sure it's doing them a lot of good.'

'I taught some of them to sew, today. I was sick and tired of their clothes hanging about them in rags, when a bit of stitching could make all the difference.'

'Were they interested?'

'The girls were, yes.'

Jeff didn't say anything but I knew what he was thinking: that teaching girls to sew was very nineteenth-century and we had moved on from there, but that he thought he had better not say it.

So I added, 'I know that patching up ragged clothing is hardly going to transform their lives. I know that the whole thing about clothing is wrapped up in culture-defined value judgements, that it serves no practical purpose, not in this country, anyway. So, I don't know, maybe we are imposing our own values on them by suggesting they could smarten up, but...'

'Not everybody values smart clothes. Some people see through it.'

'No, but I suspect they would probably love smart clothes. Anyway, I think it's good if they have the choice. And who knows? One of them might set up a business as a clothes mender.'

'Who knows? But I like it better that you're teaching them to read and write. That's where women's empowerment really lies, I'm pretty sure. In fact, it's been proved.'

'Yeah, right,' I said, cynically. 'And the demographic transition going to start right here on our veranda.'

14

Wednesday

I met Thomas, the surgeon, on his way to work this morning, as I often did. He would always greet me warmly. He would come up to me with his big mouth in full smile and grasp my hand tightly. 'Hello, Laura, and how are you today?'

I always said 'Fine.' Then he would go through the rigmarole of asking how Annabel was, and how was Jeff, and so on. We often said it in our pidgin Swahili because it was the local custom, when greeting someone, to ask not only how they were, but how was everybody and everything else. '*Na habari ya shule kidogo?*' And how was my little 'school, he asked, to which we both laughed. I always said '*Mzuri*', everything was fine.

I wished I'd been bold enough to tell him the truth, that I was fed up, homesick for family and friends, and for home comforts – all the many, many things I took for granted in England and couldn't get here. And how I felt misplaced, without a role, not that I could have accepted any job if I had found one, because of the childcare situation. And how I felt a misfit because of the cultural gap between me and the local women, and with the language problem, and so on and so on. But I never mentioned any of this to Thomas.

He probably sensed the truth, because he would always then tell me that his wife and family were coming soon, once the children's school term had finished, or that his wife just had to tidy up some affairs.

I had learned to take this lightly, because the promised arrival never happened. Sofia had insinuated that his family didn't actually exist, and that he had made them up for tax advantages, or to get a bigger house.

This time, he said 'Well, life is going to get so good, because my family are coming at last! They just have to get their flights fixed up and they will be here. And my wife, she is a good woman; you need a friend, Laura, and she will be the friend you need.'

I couldn't see how Thomas's wife was going to be the answer to everything that was getting me down, let alone believe that she was really coming at all, but I humoured him.

'That must be very exciting for you. I'm looking forward to meeting her, and all your children.'

Thursday

Sofia had lent me her juicer, but I had not yet used it. With the children coming every day, I hadn't had a chance to go to the market. This had not been a problem because plenty of people came round selling vegetables.

The vendors were not the only people who came round looking for money. Most of them simply came begging, like the man with a severed arm who pleaded that he had no money for food. I gave him the smallest note I had, which should have kept him in maize for a week, but he returned the very next day, wearing a new tee-shirt, and again asking for money. I was going to send him away, but I knew I would feel guilty. Why should he not have a new tee-shirt, after all. And if that meant he was still hungry, then he should eat.

Boys came asking for pens and other small items for school, other people tried to sell me things they couldn't possibly think I'd want to buy. One woman tried to sell me a worn straw mat for the equivalent of ten dollars. She looked so destitute and desperate I gave her the money. Onlookers signalled that I was mad to pay that much; the mat wasn't worth it.

But of course, that wasn't the point. I had always thought these so-called primitive people looked after one another, but it would appear that wasn't the case. Women were often cast out of their communities for being divorced, a state that was usually imposed upon them by their husbands, for infertility, for example. Or because they had gynaecological problems, often because of a cliterectomy that had made them incontinent, and therefore, social rejects.

Cases like these were among the many things that pulled on my heartstrings, painfully.

Other incidents were just amusing. Some children tried to sell me a tortoise. Why they would imagine I would want one? No-one here kept pets just for the sake of it. 'Is it good to eat?' I asked them, to which they rolled around in mirth.

Two women approached us to sell little girls' dresses. They were the frilly, sticky-out kind made of multiple layers of flimsy material that we used to call party dresses. Annabel wanted the pink one. Jeff said we should buy it.

Assuming the women would not understand, I uttered out loud, 'But it's hideous!' to which the vendors doubled up laughing.

Then there was Abel. He turned up at the house again, this time to tell me that his mother was ill and she needed to go to the hospital in Harare, which was a very long way away. Of course I didn't believe him. But what if it were true? People often had to suffer life-long afflictions because they couldn't afford the bus fare to go and get an operation.

Moreover, Abel had pulled me into his world; they had put on a show for me, had invited me to eat with them, had given me presents. By European standards those gifts had been tiny, but to these people on the breadline, they would not have been trivial. I had taken photographs of them which they would not be able to see for some time. Did I owe them something? They probably thought I did, now. Anyway, why be stingy? If it were true about his mother, the money for the bus fare would make all the difference. By European standards, it was not very much anyway.

Those little handouts were adding up, however. I was alarmed to find how fast the cash was running out. I had to trek to the bank yet again, and there I was reminded that I had paid eight children's school fees, even if the money had disappeared into a (hopefully temporary) black hole. The trek to town reminded me we really needed a car. All going well, we could afford one with Jeff's first salary. We had no money for one before then.

I was dealing with two sets of economics. There was day-to-day Africa in which everything seemed ridiculously cheap and we were extraordinarily rich and could afford anything and everything. But we were still products of the rich world with its culture, its expectations and its commitments. Living in London had needed both our salaries. We had sunk our savings into a flat, which we had now let, but the rent only covered the mortgage repayments. We couldn't have afforded a car back there, but we hadn't needed one. Before coming to Africa, a big chunk of our final income had gone on estate agent's fees and other upheaval costs. We hadn't seen this as a problem because we knew Africa was going to be cheap and in the long run we would do very well, financially. But there was no money for a car yet.

Actually, I was beginning to worry if there would be enough to last until payday.

Before going to the bank, I went to the market to buy fruit. One had to get there early. I would need to return Sofia's juicer and had still not used it. I bought a pineapple and some lemons. But the mangos were not in season. So how had Sofia come up with mango juice? It was yet another thing about this wonder-woman that baffled me.

After the bank, I went to buy exercise books and pencils for each of the children who were coming to our informal 'school'. It made sense to do things properly, if they were not able to go to school before next term.

I would have bought more materials, but found nothing more in the shops. There were some basic sewing things, and I bought these. I was teaching the skill to whoever wanted to learn it.

Back at the house I got to work making juice. I had never used a juicer before; I hadn't needed one, because in London you could pick up a vast range of fruit juices in every flavour, form and price-range from the corner shop. Anyway, I assumed I only had to chop up the fruit, throw it in and switch it on, which is what I did.

The machine ground away noisily for several minutes, without seeming to produce much liquid. Then it came to a sickening halt. I dismantled it and cleaned it and tried again. Nothing.

Damn! This is just typical. Of all the people I could have borrowed it from!

I put it away and hoped Jeff could fix it.

Jeff couldn't fix the juicer.

'What will I do?' I moaned. 'There's no way I can replace it. There won't be another one for thousands of miles.'

'Get her one of those plastic lemon-grinder things.'

'Don't be ridiculous! I'll have to offer to pay for it. And I have no idea how much these things cost. A fortune, including shipping, most likely.'

'Do that then. Don't worry about it.'

I thought I had better offer Sofia about two hundred pounds to replace it. If it cost less than that she would surely tell me. I went over to her place straightaway.

15

Roy answered the door. He invited me in. I explained why I'd come.

'Sofia's been called out to the hospital,' he said. 'She probably won't be very long. You can wait for her if you like. Or I can pass on the message.'

I didn't feel comfortable with Roy, partly because of his higher status, but mostly because he always seemed so stern, even angry. He did not look the sort to indulge in small-talk.

However, I thought the situation warranted a personal apology to Sofia. I said I'd wait.

Roy offered me a drink and I accepted. It would help avoid an awkward silence.

He sat down at the table with me. 'How are you getting on with the patients' records system?' he asked.

'Well, I'm doing what we agreed. I just hope it will be good enough…'

'You know, Laura, I think it's really good that you're doing this. If we can get a functioning system going it could really improve the quality of care. Sofia, and all the doctors really, think it can't be done without computers, but even if we had them we'd have to employ a database expert. Do you know how much they cost? A fortune!'

'Well, this system won't be anything like as good…'

'It will be much better than nothing, and it will stop Sofia nagging at me to invest money we don't have in computers. She would insist on an expensive one. She's so extravagant, it's crippling.'

I was taken aback by his openness to me about his wife. I searched for something ameliorating to say, but he seemed to read my thoughts, and pre-empted it.

'Don't get me wrong. She is a good doctor. She's great with the kids, but…'

'I was surprised to find someone like Sofia here in Africa, where there's so much poverty. I would have expected her to want to be somewhere well-resourced.'

Roy leaned closer towards me. 'But she loves it here. Where else would she be able to live in a house like this – this majestic Roman palace, with all these servants, playing the role of benevolent queen to all those poor people around us? Certainly not in England. She revels in it. She's from a very poor background, in Taranto, right down in the foot of Italy, and, in a way, she identifies with the local people here.'

'Oh! She told me she was from Milan.'

Roy looked surprised for a moment. 'She went to university in Milan. She was clever enough, and determined enough, to pull herself out of the poverty trap. Now she does her best to distance herself from it all. Or at least, she has to keep proving to herself that she's come up in the world.'

'Where did you and Sofia meet?' It just came out. It was the same question, that I had thought impertinent, that Sofia had asked of me and Jeff on our first night, and for the same reason. How could someone like Sofia have possibly got together with someone like Roy? I didn't doubt her ability to become a doctor. But their personalities were like oil and water.

'I was her supervisor when she was doing her intern, before she specialised.'

It made sense. The attraction of the high-status male. This stern, aloof, Darcy-like character would have been held in awe by the junior staff. Sofia would have enjoyed winning the trophy. A good-looking one, I surmised. Looking beyond furrows and worry-lines, I saw his strong jaw and well-defined brow. He had been handsome once.

'Sorry,' he said. 'I shouldn't be talking to you about my wife, not like this. She has many excellent qualities…'

'I must say I find her extremely impressive – she's amazing, really – she has such an important – and difficult job, and she seems to cope so well with it, then she's a fantastic cook on top of all that...'

'She makes a point of giving a good impression. That's very important to her. Anyway, let me get you another drink.'

I didn't need one but I let him. I wasn't sure what to say, now that he had invited me to see Sofia in a new light. I was flattered that he had confided in me. I was tempted to tell him this, but it felt inappropriate.

I was spared from making any further comment, as just then, Sofia returned from the hospital. 'Oh, hello, Laura, how lovely to see you.'

'Did you manage to save the boy?' Roy asked her.

'No, he died,' Sofia replied, matter-of-factly.

I understood this mentality. Doctors had to deal with grim situations, including death, all the time, especially here, and they would be worn down with grief if they didn't detach themselves emotionally from their work.

'So how are you, Laura,' she asked me.

I explained about breaking the juicer and that I wanted to pay for it. I handed over a wad of notes, the equivalent of two hundred pounds.

'Oh, no, don't worry,' she said.

'No, please let me pay for it. I feel so bad. Especially when you won't be able to replace it easily.'

I was hoping she would tell me I had given her far too much, but she didn't. 'Really, you shouldn't have,' she said, leaving the money where I had put it.

Friday

Our money was running out and we still had another week to go before payday. This annoyed me, because Jeff, in soft-talking me into coming to Africa, had persuaded me that that we would have far more money than we would ever need.

It was doubly annoying because it was entirely my fault that we now had to worry. Or rather, that I had to worry. Jeff had not needed to think about finances at all; hardly a shilling had crossed his palm since we had arrived. I was the one who had been over-liberal with those fat bundles of notes of next-to-no value.

Now I had to wonder whether I really should be feeding all those other children. More and more had joined us every day. The cost of vegetables here was so low that it had hardly seemed to matter, however much I bought. They were brought to the door, and Mary and some of the girls did the cooking.

But in terms of food-buying ability, I had handed over a vast fortune to Sofia to replace her juicer, and now I would have to cut back on even those cheaper-than-cheap vegetables.

When the vendor came to the door, I told him I didn't have enough money. He didn't seem at all surprised at this, as I thought he might. He offered them to me for half the price.

How could he afford to do that, here, where people lived so much on the edge? Had he been overcharging me all along? Probably. I had to give it to him.

Anyway, I couldn't turn the children away hungry. Feeding them felt like the one useful thing I could do. I let them eat as soon as we could get the vegetable stew ready. They seemed to concentrate on the lessons so much better when their stomachs were no longer empty.

Most of them did, anyway. It was not the case with Salome, who always appeared doleful and languid. She looked and behaved much younger than her fourteen years.

She liked playing with dolls most of all. This morning, before she left she was particularly reluctant to part with Rosie, Annabel's ragdoll. I didn't want to let her have it because Annabel was especially fond of this one. Besides, she had given a little black doll to Salome the day before.

I had not been sure whether to praise my daughter for her generosity, or regret that she had not much valued the dark-skinned doll. I had bought it for her shortly before coming to Africa in the hopes of engendering in her an attitude that babies were to be loved, whatever the colour of their skin. However, it seemed that she did not cherish Susie, the black doll as much as the pink-skinned, yellow pigtailed Rosie. And neither, it would appear, did Salome. It stuck in my throat that racial attitudes were obviously so deeply ingrained.

It annoyed me too, that I had to coerce Salome into handing back the doll. I felt mean, and resented that she made me feel this way. They wanted so much; they needed so much. One could not stop feeling guilty until you had given them the shirt off your back.

'What happened to the doll we gave you yesterday,' I asked Salome.

'It's leg broke,' she replied, her eyes rolling in sadness while still clutching Rosie. The whites of her eyes were yellow. It was because she had sickle-cell anaemia, Sofia had told me. This genetic disease affected many Sub-Saharan Africans and condemned them to a short life of bad health. It had probably taken its toll on Salome's development.

I gently removed the doll from her arms. 'Come, Salome, have another bowl of stew.' The least I could do was to get some decent food into her.

16

Saturday

And then at last it happened. Thomas's family arrived. They came after dark, as we had, but unlike us, they didn't seem in the least worn out from the five-hour drive along rough tracks after their flight. There were shouts and yelps and laughter. They made no secret of the fact that this Nigerian family was overjoyed to be reunited. We, and everyone else emerged from our houses to see what the racket was about.

'Jeff and Laura, meet my wife, Miriam – Doctor and Mrs Whitely, Wittley, ha ha.'

Miriam shook our hands vigorously. 'I am very happy to meet you, Laura. I have heard so much about you, and how you are so good with all the children. And now, Sister, we bring you another six!' She laughed, her ample breasts heaving. She was a big lady in all dimensions, tall, wide, big hands, big laugh, big voice. I got the feeling she had a big heart, too.

'And these are our children.' She shouted to them. 'Ester, Apara, Ewansiha, Jumoke, Obataiye, Madu, come here and be introduced.'

I was never going to remember any of those names. None of them could be summoned, anyway. They were all over the place, exploring the compound, the swimming pool, their new house, calling out to each other whenever they came across something exciting, which seemed to be all the time. I had no idea what language they were speaking, although their mother had spoken to them in English.

Of course, Sofia held a party for them, that very evening. As when we had first arrived, she introduced the new arrivals theatrically, although she needed prompting with the children's names. Miriam responded equally dramatically. She had brought the post with her, and now she ceremoniously handed out the letters that were addressed to individuals.

'Mrs Okoye,' said Edward. 'You should have brought the post straight to me at the hospital administration office, These letters are confidential.'

'These are only the personal letters,' Miriam asserted. 'Of course, I will bring the hospital post straight to you.'

'You should not have looked into the bag,' Edward retaliated. 'It is the property of the hospital.'

Miriam went over and put her arm around the hospital administrator's shoulders.

'Brother,' she said. 'Are you grateful to me for bringing the post, or not?'

'Yes, of course I am grateful,' Edward muttered.

There was a letter for me, addressed in my mother's handwriting. What a lovely surprise! Considering the circuitous route the mail had to go by, I could not reasonably have expected a letter to reach me within the first month, if at all. Although I had managed to send one to my parents it would certainly not have arrived before they posted this one. I could hardly wait for a chance to slip away and read it. But now was not the time.

Miriam explained that she was a business lady and that it had taken these six months to get her affairs in order and arrange for the shipment of her merchandise.

'What do you sell?' I asked her.

'Bed nets, condoms, soap, paper towels, sanitary towels. That is my merchandise.'

'Quite an assortment, then.'

'But sister, these are the things that are most important for the health of the community. No matter how clever your doctors are, no matter how much expensive medicine, or how much fancy equipment you've got, it is these basic things that save people's lives the most, and keeps them free of disease.'

Could it really have been that simple? I doubted it. If it was, surely Africa's problems would have been solved before now.

'How are you going to sell condoms?' asked Roy. 'It's bad enough trying to get men to persuade other men to use them at all. They're not going to buy them from a woman.'

'I am not going to sell them to men,' answered Miriam. 'I am going to sell them to women. The women need to empower themselves. It is the women who must take responsibility for their own bodies. Now, what we really need are female condoms, which would not even need the co-operation of a man. I wish someone would invent those. Now, that would be real progress.'

'There exist already female condoms,' said Philippe. 'But they are not well-known. Someone has invented such a thing. But I do not think they could ever be successful. It would not work.'

'Well, Doctor Laval, I want to know where I can get some of those.'

I was hardly the centre of attention, so I took the chance to sneak back to my own house and read my letter.

I trembled with excitement as I opened it.

Dear Laura,

Well, it is now a whole week since you left. I hope you all arrived safe and sound. We were hoping you would phone when you got there. I know you said the phones don't work out there, but we didn't really believe you, but I suppose that's the reason you didn't. Not much has been happening here. The weather has been pretty miserable, although we have been keeping well enough, apart from the usual grumbles, which we won't bore you with.

What's it like out there? I imagine it's very hot. Do you have air-conditioning? I dare say you're living the life of Larry, sunbathing by the pool and having servants to do all the housework, but I must say, there's hardly a day goes by when we don't worry about you, especially our granddaughter. How is she? Is she getting enough to eat?

Every night we see all the terrible things that happen in Africa, like all the wars, and the people starving, and we just pray that you are managing to keep away from all that kind of trouble.

Please make sure Annabel doesn't go near any danger. Are there lions near you? Have you found some nice friends with children for Annabel to play with? Don't let her near the natives, will you? Because you just never know.

What shops do you have out there? I expect there's a Marks&Sparks. They're everywhere these days. What are the prices like? I want to send Annabel a parcel. I know you said sending parcels won't work but that can't be right. Anyway, I don't want to pay a fortune for postage if you can get everything there quite cheap anyway.

How's Jeff getting on at the hospital? We are full of admiration for him going out to help the poor people of Africa, but I do wonder why he has to help bring even more babies into the world, to people who can't afford to feed themselves, just giving themselves another mouth to feed.

Anyway, it's not for me to judge. But I am sure he could get a job here if he wanted. The hospitals in Northampton need good doctors too. Even if Jeff doesn't want to come home, I daresay he could get by without you.

Remember, Laura, if you and Annabel ever want to come home, your bedroom is still waiting for you. You could even get a job in Northampton and we would look after Annabel. She should be going to school soon anyway. Are there good schools out there?

You could even go back to college if you wanted, and learn something useful.

Well, do look after yourselves, won't you? We worry terribly.

Love Mum and Dad

I read the letter through twice, then I crumpled it up and threw it into the waste bin. My throat was tightening. I pulled the letter back out of the bin, smoothed out the pages, and put them under a book. Then I blew my nose and went back to the party.

17

Friday

With mind-numbing efficiency, Miriam had put all but her youngest child in school the very first day after arriving, she had Madu, her youngest, fixed up with a minder, and had gone into town before we were even up.
I startled when I first saw the girl.
'Hope! You're back!'
'I'm not Hope,' the girl laughed. 'I'm Faith, her sister.

Unfortunately, Faith proved to be no more reliable than Hope. She would leave Madu with us for the morning, which was all right; one more child didn't make much difference. But by the end of the morning Faith was often nowhere to be found, and I would be stuck with the three-year-old. Then the other five would come home from school and play at our house, and I would still be the only adult around.

'Thank you so much, Laura. I knew the children would be in good hands,' Miriam said when she came home around five on the first day.
I told her about Faith, but whatever she said to the girl did not make any difference. Her presence was erratic and I was left with Madu most of the time.
I decided not to push it with Miriam, however. The children, including Annabel, clearly welcomed the new arrivals, even if I was less than happy.
Those Nigerian kids were wild! They darted around in all directions, bouncing balls off every surface, all chattering at once in loud excited voices in some dialect of English I

couldn't decipher. I couldn't remember their names, either, which made it even less possible to control them.

Often, they would spontaneously start drumming. Every hollow object around was upturned and became an instrument. They even brought out all the saucepans and wooden spoons from the kitchen. 'You might have asked first,' I said to them, but not one of them took any notice.

But boy, could they drum! This rhythmic beating was obviously second nature to them. The local kids would join in, and everybody who wasn't drumming would dance to the beat. Those moments were euphoric.

Annabel loved those exuberant kids, but they gave her problems too. Once, a number of her toys went missing, giving us a prolonged and anguished search. It was irritating because I couldn't just go shopping and replace them.

I wanted to warn the children that if we couldn't trust them we couldn't let them play at our place. However, my Swahili wasn't up to it, and I reluctantly recruited Sofia into giving them the lecture. She had felt sure it would have been the Nigerian children's doing. I had felt it wrong of her to be prejudiced. None the less, we eventually did find the toys in the house of the new family.

'Well, we all know about Nigerians,' said Jeff, imitating Sofia, when I told him about it. He found it amusing that she repeatedly dismissed all Nigerians as a bunch of crooks.

I told Miriam about it that evening and she gave her kids such a bawling out, I wondered whether I should go and protect them from her. However, I also knew enough about her boys already. Water and ducks' backs came to mind.

I envied the speed with which Miriam settled in. She had learned some Swahili before coming, and she eased herself into the community and established connections within no time. Her capability made me feel pathetic in comparison, but I also benefited from it.

For example, she was good at sourcing various foodstuffs which I had assumed were not available. On that Thursday, she had brought us a huge chunk of game meat. One of her instantly-made acquaintances had been out hunting and had shot a wildebeest. Jeff and I were not great meat-eaters but it certainly made a nice change from beans and vegetable stew. We ate it all in one go.

Sunday

For some days now, we had been down to our last few shillings. This would barely keep us in basic foodstuffs until payday, which was Monday. As we usually did on Sundays, we spent Jeff's only day off around the house. He was happy to do this because he was worn out after a long hard week, and it was a nice change for him to do the things that I did with Annabel every day, like walking around *shambas*, saying *Jambo* to the villagers, and playing with the children. After being called Dr Wittley, or sometimes Whitely, all week, he enjoyed his village name, *Baba Annabel*. Or we would sit on one veranda or another, and have endless debates about healthcare in Africa.

I had been looking forward to doing all the exciting things Europeans usually came to Africa for. There was a safari park three hours drive away, and a beautiful rainforest not far away with colobine monkeys and waterfalls, apparently, and one could go on canoe trips on the river outside town and see hippopotamuses, we had heard.

Sofia and Roy had taken off this weekend on one such holiday, but with no car and no money left, we couldn't do that. Jeff had shown no inclination to take any time out, anyway. His way of coping with his guilt for the huge disparity in fortune between us and the local people was to keeping working. Perhaps he felt he needed to atone for the unfairness, and didn't deserve any pleasure in the face of so much suffering. More likely, he simply thought he had better get on with dealing with it all.

I was fed up. I felt rotten about venting my woes onto Jeff, but I moaned to him nevertheless. 'All the others give themselves time off for pleasure trips. Why can't we? You're supposed to get a long weekend once a month, aren't you?'

'Well, we need to think about getting a car. Then we could maybe think about taking a weekend off. Wait until my queues die down a bit, first.'

'Die down? Ha ha.'

'We have to wait till I get paid, anyway, don't we?'

'We certainly do. And until then it's beans again for supper,'

'Hey, I know,' said Jeff. 'Sofia said we could go over to theirs and watch a video. Why don't we do that tonight?'

It seemed like a good idea, so after our mundane meal we went over.

Not surprisingly, Sofia and Roy had a vast selection of videos, although on closer inspection, there was not much that appealed to us. Most of them were obviously for their children.

We chose *Babette's Feast*, which was written by Karen Blixen, renowned for *Out of Africa*, so it seemed appropriate.

This story is not set in Africa but in a remote, drab village in 19th century Denmark. After a lifetime devoid of pleasure, two puritanical Christian sisters are visited upon by Babette, a French refugee, who prepares the banquet of a lifetime for the members of their tiny church. The rest of the film treats the viewers to a visual feast of mouth-watering dishes.

Having had a frugal plate of beans for supper, however, the culinary delights on film served more to torture our tastebuds than enrapture them. It didn't help that we were sitting in a house we had come to associate with sumptuous dinner parties, and we knew that if we cared to look in

Sofia's fridge, we would most likely find food to satisfy our wildest desires. But we knew we should not look, and we came away hungrier than ever.

Monday

I did borrow a bottle of wine from Sofia. We had something to celebrate. Today was payday. I could hardly wait till Jeff came home. My relief was going to be profound.

'Well, did you get your salary?' I asked, when the moment finally arrived.

'No, it hasn't come through,' Jeff replied.

I knew all along that it could never have happened so smoothly. My heart sank, nonetheless

. 'What do you mean it hasn't come through? When will it come through?'

'I don't know. Nobody knows. Maybe tomorrow.'

'What about our trip to the safari park next weekend?'

'I'd rather wait until the pay comes through. Money's getting tight, isn't it?'

'Yes!' I couldn't conceal my annoyance.

But I said nothing more. This was Africa, I had to remember. Things couldn't work efficiently. It would be bad form to complain when everyone else had it so much worse.

18

Monday

Another whole week passed and Jeff had still not been paid. My spirits sank lower and my patience grew thinner every time he came home empty-handed. My wallet also grew thinner. There was no point in going to the bank this Monday morning, as I usually did. I had emptied our account well before the end of the month.

The children came to the house as usual, but today I had to tell them there was nothing to eat. I felt horrible about this. I guessed that their parents had come to rely on me feeding them, and felt spared from the responsibility themselves. So, although I was keeping some food back for ourselves, the children were left to go hungry. This made them ill-tempered, and the day passed miserably.

But the evening was a whole lot worse. An unwelcome visitor came straight into our house, through the front door without a *Hodi*. We had left it open, foolishly, in retrospect.

It was already getting dark, but typically for a Monday, Jeff was not yet home. Somehow, the intruder had evaded the security man at the gate, if he was there. The compound was surrounded by a high wall, and unsolicited entry should not have been possible. But there it was. Annabel was beside me, so I was able to grab her hand and whisper to her. 'Stay very still and don't make a sound.'

She obeyed me. Perhaps she sensed the fear in my voice, although I tried not to let it show. Perhaps the tightness with which I gripped her hand relayed the urgency of the message. Perhaps she was paralysed. Or perhaps she wasn't frightened at all. She seemed to have inherited Jeff's tendency to take everything in his stride. That might have been a good thing on some occasions, but this was definitely not one of them. On the other hand, I was very glad she didn't scream.

Maybe that was because there was something comical about the face; the big wide smiling mouth and large shining eyes, reminiscent of *The Muppets*, and suggesting friendliness. But for me, this paradox added to the nightmare quality of the experience. It was a mocking expression, as if speaking for the whole of Africa: *So, Mrs Whitelady, you want to be so kind and generous towards us; you think you can sort out all our problems, do you? Well, just let me show you what we would really like from you.*

Our visitor was a brownish-olive colour rather than black, but I was in no doubt about the identity, because I had read up about the dangers one might encounter in Sub-Saharan Africa, and I recognised this one as one of the worst possible. One wrong move and one of us would be dead.

The black mamba is the fastest snake in the world, capable of moving at 4 to 5 metres a second. It can grow up to 14 feet and can raise one third of its body off the ground. Its venom is virulently toxic and is deadly to a human adult. But it is shy and secretive; it always seeks to escape when a confrontation occurs. However, if cornered, it may strike repeatedly.

One should never ever attack a snake, nor turn one's back on it. Instead one should stay motionless...

I had no guarantee that neither of us would make a wrong move. I desperately wanted to scream. Annabel would have no idea how dangerous it was. How long could my tight grip convey the crucial message? *Don't move! Don't speak!*

...and if it does not go away, one should slowly step backwards...

There was no way to step backwards; our backs were against the wall. We might have been able to step sideways, but would this have been a good move? I had no idea. In any case, I was frozen to the spot.

If a black mamba comes into the house, it is best to throw a cover over it, under which it will calm down. One should secure the blanket with weights so that it does not escape, then go and seek help.

I could not do this. There was no blanket within reach, as far as I knew, and I dared not turn my head to look for something. I longed for Jeff to come home, or for anyone to come and help, yet I knew that the sound of someone approaching could startle the snake into action. We were gridlocked. Either we would have to stay like this for ever or something would cause the snake to strike. Or maybe we could hope it would go away. I willed telepathy to work.

Go away, snake. Just go away now please. I repeated this in my head over and over. *Go away, snake. Just go away now please.* I hoped that Annabel could hear me inside her head. I recanted the mantra over and over.

An eternity passed. *Why are you not coming home, Jeff? Has something happened to you? Is there another snake out there? Or have you gone for a drink, or something? When you do eventually come, you will find us both dead, and that will teach you.*

Teach him what? I was appalled that I was about to leave this world with angry thoughts about my beloved husband.

If I am going to leave this world, my very last thoughts should be - should be... I had no idea what they should be; I could hardly think at all.

A choking noise came from my throat.

I was aghast. That was surely the end.

Then the snake left. It just turned and slithered off, the way it came in.

I waited a few seconds to let it get well out of the way, then I went over and slammed the door shut, which, I knew, was the wrong thing to do because it could have startled the snake into attack.

Shuddering, I rushed back over to my daughter, hugged her tight and burst into sobs.

But relief didn't come. How many ways were there for a snake to get into the house? I searched the floor for holes. There were none that seemed large enough, but just how small a hole could a snake get through? I would never be able to relax again. I hated this place.

In my anguish I had forgotten that Jeff would be coming home any minute, and that outside in the dark there was a dangerous snake he might well tread upon. I realised it just as he came in. I had never felt more relieved to see him.

'Oh Jeff, you'll never guess! We had a snake in the house. I'm sure it was a black mamba.'

Jeff came over and put his arms around me. 'Hey, calm down,' he said. 'What makes you think it was a black mamba. Are you sure you weren't just imagining it?'

'I was definitely not imagining it!'

'But it wasn't black, Mummy, it was brown.' Annabel turned to her father. 'But it had a black mouth.'

'Did it?' For once, Jeff looked worried. His eyes darted around the room.

'Yes,' Annabel continued. 'So we had to be very quiet and wait for it to go away.'

Jeff sat down and pulled his daughter onto his lap. He nestled her head under his chin. 'You were very brave, Annabel.'

I sat down and gulped. I wanted to shout out, *What about me?*

Of course, there was no point.

I did say, 'Well, I'm glad you didn't step on it outside.'

'You've got a good point,' said Jeff, getting up again. 'We should tell the security man about it. I wonder how it got in. And we should keep the doors shut at night,' he added as he went out.

'Take a torch,' I urged him. I sat down again and let the tears flow down my cheeks. *I can't cope with this place.*

Tuesday

When the children came the next morning they were all talking excitedly and rapidly. I had no idea what they were saying.

Then Annabel said to them, 'It came in our house.'

Everyone stopped in surprise, including myself, but my own surprise was for a different reason from the children's. They had been talking in Swahili and Annabel had understood them.

Nyoka? Katika nyumba? they asked.

Annabel nodded.

'What are they talking about, Annabel?'

Miki wiggled his finger to signify a snake. 'Bwana Songoro.' He pointed out to the courtyard, and mimed the action of capturing something.

Bwana Songora was the security guard. He had captured the snake.

And Annabel could understand Swahili.

This should have been a joyful discovery. I should have marvelled at her cleverness and her willingness to learn. I should have been relieved that our communication problems would be lessened. Annabel would now be able to talk to the children, which meant she could take her relationships with them to a new level. She had taken a major step towards becoming integrated. Moreover, if she really was able to pick up the language faster than I could, as small children very often could, she would be able to translate for me. Life would be easier all round.

But I was not joyful at the discovery. I was too far beyond that. I was miserable and I wanted to go home. Now I was looking for things to strengthen my conviction that it was not feasible to stay here, not facts that would undermine it.

19

Tuesday evening

When Jeff came home from work and he had still not been paid, I cracked. 'It's that Edward! He's got it in for us, because I sacked his daughter! He's withholding your wages for spite!'

'I don't think so...'

'What are we going to do? The money's running out!'

'We could always bring in our savings from England...'

'What savings? We don't have any savings! And even if we did, don't you think you do enough for this goddamned place without pouring all your worldly wealth into it as well?'

'Please, Laura, calm down. I came here to help these people. I get much more satisfaction from what I do here than just filling some lucrative slot back home. You know that. We're not here for the money.'

'You can say that again! I've never heard anything so ridiculous!'

'Mummy!' Our daughter started to cry.

'Let's not argue in front of Annabel,' said Jeff, quietly. 'What have you been up to today, Annabel?'

But I could not calm down. If we had been in England I would have gone out for a walk to dissipate my fury, but this was Africa, and it was pitch black outside.

It got worse; there was a power failure and the lights went out. This was not unusual; it happened two or three times a week, but just then, it felt punishing. There was nothing else to do but go to bed.

Wednesday

My anger had not abated by morning. I tossed and turned in bed all night, churning bitter thoughts about Edward withholding the money out of sheer pettiness, or embezzling it, just because he could, and because people like Jeff let him get away with it.

I stewed in fury, but also in a sweat-bath, because with the electricity cut off, the overhead fans were not working.

By morning I had hardly slept, and I felt bad-tempered and wretched. When I got up I was rudely reminded that I had not cleared up from supper the previous evening. Cockroaches and ants were crawling over the leftover food.

Jeff had already left for work. I had wanted to discuss again the matter of not being paid before Annabel woke up, but he had quietly evaded this. Realising what he had done infuriated me even more.

There was only one thing for it. The matter had to be dealt with head on.

I went into Annabel's room and woke her up. There was no-one around to look after her this early, so she would have to come with me. Annabel didn't like being woken up abruptly, and she complained loudly, but I was in no mood to appease her.

I helped her get dressed, then looked quickly for something for her to eat and drink, but as the fridge had been off all night, the milk was already disgusting. I poured her some water, but it was warm.

'I want Agent Orange,' she said.

'OK,' I said, trying to stay calm, and opened a bottle of the fizzy drink. There was no way she could sit down to eat. I gave her a banana, which she ate standing up. I started clearing the debris from the table, but I was impatient.

I took Annabel by the hand. 'Come on, darling. We've got to go to the hospital.'

The hospital wasn't far, but Annabel was still sleepy and I was pulling her along too fast. Soon she was sobbing loudly, but I was too angry to pacify her.

I marched into the hospital administrator's office, without knocking. Edward was sitting at his desk. Surprised, he got up to greet me. 'MrsWhitely, what can I do for you?'

'You can pay my husband's salary. That's what you can do. It's already nine days late and it's high time he was paid. My husband deserves better than this.' My voice was shaking. 'Are you, by any chance, withholding his salary for your own personal ends?' My throat was tight and my fists were clenched. Annabel was still sobbing. I swallowed, and put my arm around her.

Edward took the opportunity to answer. He spoke calmly. 'MrsWhitely, are you accusing me of being a crook?'

The honest answer was 'yes'. I had certainly suspected it. But now face-to-face with the man, whose eyes had not flinched from mine, I had lost my nerve. 'Well, it's looking pretty like it,' I said, almost under my breath.

'Mrs Whitely, your husband has not been paid because his salary has not come through. His is not the only one. None of the salaries have come through. Not mine, not even the superintendent's. Ask him. This is normal. They don't come through on time because the post doesn't work, the phones don't work, we don't have computers. We don't get enough supplies, there's a shortage of drugs. Look outside; the schools don't function because the teachers don't get paid. Nothing works smoothly. We run the hospital on a shoestring, but it is thanks to people like your good husband that it carries on despite everything, that we manage to keep going. It is not how we want it, but we have no choice. This is our life. Welcome to Africa, Mrs Whitelady.

I gaped, dumbfounded. How humiliating!

But he was right, of course. I had been here five weeks already and I knew exactly how nothing worked properly.

I felt so embarrassed. No-one else complained but they all suffered, and some rather more than others. My behaviour had been shameful. Now on top of hating everything around me, I hated myself too.

I had to go and see Jeff. I needed him.

Annabel's crying had subdued to a whimper. I took her hand. 'Let's go and see Daddy,' I whispered.

I put my head round the partition that screened Dr Wittley's consulting room from the corridor. 'Can I speak to you, Jeff?'

'I've got a patient, Laura. Can you wait?'

'Please, Jeff, I must speak to you now.'

Jeff looked up and saw how distressed we were. He walked over to us. 'What's wrong?'

'I've just had a terrible row with Edward and....'

'Laura, I'm sorry, I can't deal with that now. Can't it wait? I'll see you at lunch time, OK?' Jeff returned to his patient.

I turned away in dismay. *He's angry with me; he's ashamed of me; he hates me.*

I walked past the long queue of pregnant, sick and worn-out women and their wailing children, all waiting to see my husband.

I can't cope with this place, I have failed the challenge. I am a weak and pathetic good-for-nothing, and a drain on precious resources. I should never have come. Jeff is better off without me. I should just go now, and leave him to get on with his work in peace.

I walked with Annabel back to the house.

Mary, the housemaid was there when we arrived and she had already cleaned up the mess. Seeing the crying child, she took her onto her lap and cradled her.

I went straight through to the bedroom and started throwing things into a suitcase.

Then I hastily wrote a note to Jeff. *We're going back. I'm sorry but I can't cope. I would just be a burden if I stayed. You will get on better without me.*

I closed the suitcase, picked it up and went back to the kitchen to fetch Annabel. Mary was rocking her back and forth on her lap, and they were both sobbing.

'Come, Annabel,' I said. 'We're going now.'

'Where are you going?' Mary asked in Swahili.

'Home,' I said in English. 'Come on, Annabel.' I picked up the suitcase and walked out. Mary followed, carrying Annabel. They were both still crying.

I wished I had not packed so much. The case was heavy. Out on the road, the three of us attracted much attention. Passers-by asked Mary what was happening, but I didn't understand their questions or Mary's reply. Some people tagged along. A boy came up and took the suitcase. 'Where to?' he asked.

'To the bus stop,' I told him.

There was only one bus stop. It was on the single road that led into and out of town. Annabel and I would wait there until a bus came and it would take us on the long journey into Kubwamji, the big city from where we would get a flight back to London.

20

I felt horrible about what I was doing. I knew Jeff would be heart-broken. I was taking his daughter away from him and I was depriving Annabel of her father, and of the special experience of living in Africa. Now, the two of us would face an uncertain future together as a single-parent family in dismal, depressing England.

But I felt horrible about everything. I hated myself and everybody else here, and, in fact, everything about this place. Nothing would be any better anywhere else, but I just wanted to get away.

It was embarrassing to be the focus of so much attention. Everyone around us looked very concerned. Clearly they were all aware that something was wrong, but it would be even more embarrassing if I now changed my mind and turned back. So I let the boy lead me to the bus stop, and Mary came behind with Annabel, along with our now quite large number of followers.

At the bus stop I paid the boy and sat on my case. Annabel asked repeatedly where we were going, and why, and why wasn't her Daddy coming. I had no satisfactory answers for her, and I did my best to ignore her. I was feeling very stupid now, and I just wanted to remove myself from this ridiculous situation before I started crying too. It would be a relief to get away.

In the distance, along the stretch of road I could see the bus approaching. It would arrive at the stop soon, and my suitcase would be hoisted onto the roof alongside the sacks of vegetables and all the other cargo, and I would take that pivotal step after which there was no going back: we would climb into the bus and it would drive off and we would be gone from this place forever.

As the bus pulled up, I rose from my makeshift seat, picked up the case and took my daughter from the housemaid's arms. Mary looked so miserable I could hardly look her in the face. My eyes were blurry and my throat was tight. All I could whisper was '*Asante. Kwaheri.* Thank you. Goodbye.'

Someone had taken the suitcase out of my hand. I looked up to see it being pulled onto the roof. Everyone was waiting for me to get into the bus. There was nothing more to do, nothing more to stop me from taking the irreversible action which would change my life forever.

It was awful. I couldn't do it. I had to act. It was now or never.

'Stop,' I shouted up to the men on top of the bus. I said it in English. I should have known the Swahili word, but it wouldn't come to me.

The men putting the luggage on the roof paused. They looked at me askance for a moment, then they went back to their hauling.

Had they not understood? I pointed to my suitcase. 'Bring it down again,' I called up to them. 'I've changed my mind.'

They appeared not to hear. There was much shouting going on, everyone concerned about their own affairs, not mine. The bus-driver revved his engine. Somebody was telling me to get on the bus. I looked to Mary for help, but she was sobbing. It was hopeless. It was too late. I was doing a terrible thing and now it was irrevocable. All I could do was succumb.

Someone was trying to take Annabel out of my arms to carry her onto the bus.

'No!' I shouted it. I had never heard my voice so loud before. I tightened my grip of Annabel and shouted again. 'No! I'm not going!'

They had heard me. Now there was a hush. All eyes were upon me. I felt so stupid. But I had to go through with it. 'Bring my case down,' I yelled to the men on the roof.

This time they understood. I watched them lower my case to the ground, wondering how on Earth I was going to face the embarrassment of walking back.

'Mama Annabel! I suspected I might find you here. What do you think you are doing?'

It was Miriam, She marched up to me. Faith followed, along with a number of others who had tagged along.

I could maintain my façade of composure no longer. 'I was going back to England,' I said, my voice breaking, and the tears finally rolling. 'I feel no use here. Jeff would get on better without me.'

'Mama Annabel, you are going nowhere. You're home is here. You are Dr Whitely's wife, you are Annabel's mother, you are the children's schoolmistress and you are my friend, and we cannot do without you.'

Miriam picked up my suitcase, and turned and walked back the way she came. I had no option but to follow. I wanted to argue that there was no way I could be considered a schoolmistress, but words failed me, and Miriam wasn't listening anyway.

A vehicle pulled up beside us. Miriam's husband, Thomas was driving, and beside him was Jeff.

He got out and flung his arms around me and Annabel and buried his face in my shoulder. He sobbed, 'Laura, we've found you! I'm so relieved! You've no idea how much we've worried. I need you so much. Please don't ever leave me.'

'I won't,' I said, wiping my tears.

We climbed into the car, along with Faith, Mary, and as many of the hangers-on that could be squeezed in.

135

When we got back to the house Jeff put his arms around me again. 'We need to talk. You've given me a terrible shock. I've been neglecting you, I realise that now.'

I shook my head. I've been the selfish one. Giving everybody all this trouble, pulling you away from all your patients. I'd better let you get back to work now.'

'We'll talk at lunchtime, OK?' said Jeff. He hesitated before going. 'But, please, Laura, are you going to be all right?'

I nodded.

He turned to go. 'But, oh! You should come down to the hospital. Edward says he's got something for you.'

'I think Laura needs a cup of tea first.' Miriam was standing behind us. 'Edward, and whatever he's got can wait.'

Miriam was right. I was grateful for the tea. I was calming down but the tears were still rolling.

'Laura,' she said. 'I think you and I need to talk. You have not been a happy woman of late. Am I not right?'

I nodded. 'I've been finding it hard to cope,' I said, holding the warm cup to my chin.

I told her all about our money problems and how I had been handing out donations to everyone who asked, out of guilt that they were so poor and we Europeans were so rich in comparison, and that it was the legacy of how the colonialists had treated Africans that was now giving them so many problems, and how I personally felt so helpless.

'But Laura, your husband is a doctor, and that is why you are here. He has come to provide a service that the people desperately need, and no-one here can do. And you have come to support him. Without his family, Doctor Whitely would very likely not have come. Your presence is essential, and everything else you do for this place is a bonus. And Good God, you do plenty!'

Miriam waved her hand to the world outside. 'They get plenty of bonus. But if you give them everything you have, so that you are left with nothing and cannot survive, then Doctor Whitely cannot do his work and the people have no obstetrician.' She flung her hands in the air, as if to say it was all perfectly clear.

I smiled. It was not as straightforward as that. But I accepted her point. One could not take the entirety of Africa's problems onto ones' shoulders.

'I suppose there's a fine balance between looking after your own welfare and assuaging your guilt,' I said.

'Your guilt is your own problem. You don't need it. You need to look after yourself more, Laura, or how are you going to look after your husband, or Annabel, or even those children that come to you every day?'

'Well, I meant acting on one's conscience, rather than alleviating one's guilt. There isn't much one person can do, anyway, I suppose.'

Miriam sighed. She had no time for guilt. 'You need to stand up for yourself. You need to learn assertiveness. Now, you have finished your tea. Why don't you go and see what Edward has for you. I think I know.'

We exchanged conspiratorial looks. I got up to go. She was being a bit bossy, but maybe she was right about assertiveness. It gave me an idea.

'Oh, Miriam, may I ask you a favour? Could we borrow your car one weekend soon. We want to visit the safari park.'

Miriam's mouth fell open. She had not expected such a big request from me. 'Why, of course you may,' she said, nonetheless.

Annabel, who had been cuddling me all this time,

jumped on hearing this. 'And can Madu come too?' she asked.

I heard alarm bells ringing. If I was not careful, the whole village would be coming along. If I had to learn to be assertive, why not start right here? 'No, not this time,' I said.

21

The hospital administrator looked cheerful when I walked into his office for the second time that day. 'Yes,' he said. 'At last! Your husband's salary has finally come through.' He picked up the phone and spoke in Swahili. Then he beamed. 'Go and see my secretary next door. She will give it to you.'

I went through. I startled when I saw the young woman at the desk. 'Hope!' I cried out. 'No, Faith!'

She laughed. 'I'm not Hope or Faith. I'm their sister. Charity.' She held out her hand.

'Pleased to meet you, Charity,' I said, politely.

'So, here are your husband's wages. They have finally come through.' She handed me an envelope.

'Thank you,' I said, taking it gratefully. 'You are very kind.'

'Not at all,' said Charity. 'Your husband deserves it. He is a good doctor.'

I opened the envelope straightaway and examined its contents. It was all as expected. The pay would be in the bank.

I went straight over to where Jeff was working. 'I've got it,' I called, waving the packet. He turned to me and gave a thumbs-up.

As I walked back past the queue I jumped. Yet again was that familiar face.

'Hope! What are you doing here?'

Hope got up to greet me. 'I'm pregnant,' she smiled, patting her abdomen.

'Oh, I'm so pleased for you! When is the baby due?'

'September.'

I did a quick calculation. That meant that during our first week, Hope had been two months pregnant, and quite possibly, it had been making her sick, tired, preoccupied, worried.

I was about to ask her who the father was, but thought the better of it.

'You will have your baby in the hospital, won't you?'

'Of course.'

I put my hand on her shoulder. 'I'm sure Dr Wittley will look after you very well.'

My step was lighter as I walked back to the house. What a difference that pay packet made to my mood. Minus the London allowance, Jeff's salary was the same as he had been getting in England. But here our housing was free, we had no commuting costs, food was much cheaper, and there was nothing much else to buy. And atrociously, Jeff's pay was not taxed. We were rich.

And yet, I had thought we were rich before. The wealth gap had seemed so obscenely large that I had felt there was no limit to how much I could, and should, alleviate the poverty of those around me. But there had been a limit. We would have to plan our spending in future.

'You look an awful lot happier now than you were a couple of hours ago,' said Jeff when he came home at lunchtime. 'Are you all right now?'

'I'm fine. It's such a relief. But, isn't it amazing that Edward could just come up with the money? This morning he went on and on at me about how strapped for cash they were at the hospital. Is he a crook, or what?'

'There's no evidence he's a crook. Some might call him a chancer. Others might say he's just playing the system. He would probably say he had to do a juggling act, to cover too many needs with too little money.'

'But that money was not his to play with. Your pay comes from England!'

'Anyway, you've got it now.'

'I suppose, looking on the bright side, it has been a valuable experience. Now I know what it feels like to be desperately poor.'

'Hmmm,' said Jeff doubtfully. 'Maybe, in a Marie-Antoinette-the-milkmaid-play-acting sort of way. I mean you always knew that pay-packet was coming soon.'

'It felt pretty damn real to me!'

Over lunch we worked out a financial plan. We had far more money than we needed here, yet we were surrounded by people who had not nearly enough. We would have to hold some money back for contingencies and bills back home, but we agreed that we should not refuse requests for money. However, there were limits. We needed to have a policy worked out in advance, rather than be put on the spot.

Paying the school fees of a few children had been a mistake. Jeff had correctly pointed out that there were millions of children whose parents couldn't afford the fees. However, now that I had committed to paying some, I had got myself into an awkward corner. At least, I could carry on providing some 'schooling' in our yard, until the government policy changed, if ever.

'And I'm still going to give these children a bowl of vegetable stew every day. I think it makes all the difference to the children, and it won't break the bank. And I can still hand out small things like pens and exercise books to whoever asks.'

We agreed that it would be unfair to give big things to individuals because we couldn't do it for everyone. We would make a donation to the school, for desks and chairs and a blackboard etcetera, but not a watch for the timekeeper.

'I think we should keep something for times when we feel like giving up on Africa, because I bet there'll be some.

We need sweeteners, things to look forward to, like weekends away,' I said.

'Do you think you deserve it?'

I sighed. 'Not any more than anybody else around here.' I felt my heart sink. How far should one's altruism stretch? Could I really live as frugally as most people around here, when we had the choice not to?

No, I could not, I decided. I would go mad. Or I would up sticks and leave when things got hard. I knew I would, because, unlike most people here, I could.

'Look,' I said, 'I'm not a saint. We're going to give ourselves treats, OK? Oh yes, and I've asked Miriam if we can borrow her car to go to the Safari Park next weekend. You're due a long weekend; I think we should go.'

'That's me told. But I daresay we can afford a car now.'

'Maybe, yet, you know, I've kind of got used to walking about the village, and it feels good to be down there on the ground, so to speak, with the ordinary people. Driving everywhere would distance ourselves from them.'

'Nice to have the choice, though, isn't it?' said Jeff, getting up to go back to work.

'Oh, Jeff,' I said. 'Isn't it great that you can come home at lunchtime? Not like London!'

Sofia and Roy came back from their short holiday that afternoon. I met Sofia in the swimming pool.

'Laura!' she said. 'Congratulations for standing up to that Edward. I didn't think you had it in you.'

'It was a matter of needs-musts.'

'It was high time someone did that. He's always doing that with the money. I can't stand him. He's such a slippery fellow.' She made a wiggling movement with her finger.

'Oh! And the snake! I heard! How brave you must have been. And Annabel too! I would have died.'

I was about to say she would have charmed the snake into her oven, but she had climbed out of the pool, and now she performed the most elegant dive back into the water, which hardly rippled in her wake.

Before we got out, I thought I'd better mention the record-sorting I had been doing for her.

'Oh! You don't need to worry about that anymore. I got a new computer when we were away.'

My eyes narrowed. Normally I would have stewed in silence. Today I felt the need to be different. Holding her gaze, I said, 'So I've been wasting my time, then?'

'Oh!' I had taken her aback. 'Not at all, Laura,' she said, climbing out. 'The other doctors will appreciate it, I'm sure. Roy will be delighted. And you can help me get the data onto my computer.'

I thought for a moment before I replied. 'Maybe. If I find the time. It's difficult when I've got all these children coming every day.'

Sofia dried herself in silence. Her movements seemed jerkier than usual. I lay back in the water and watched. Her body was not as beautiful as I had assumed. Middle-age was taking its toll. Her flesh was slightly saggy, and cellulite was settling into her thighs. I wondered how someone like Sofia would cope with the ingress of visual imperfection.

She finished drying herself and tied a lawn-cotton sarong under her arms.

'That's another thing I find so wonderful about you, Laura. You're so good with those kids, providing them with an education when the school doesn't function. And that's something else you could do. You should tell our friend, Wilfie, to get the schools working again. You'd be good at that. I'll sit you next to him at the next dinner party.'

She meant the British dignitary who had come previously. Despite his ineffectual demeanour, he had substantial power over the affairs of the country. I smiled at the thought of me influencing the national education policy.

'Well, I could show him a thing or two,' I said, half-seriously.

I watched Sofia stroll back to her house, her floaty sarong wafting behind her.

'She and I share some common ground,' I mused, 'even if she is better dressed.'

Sunday

Jeff and I decided to give a party that weekend. 'Let us look after the catering,' Sofia had said.

So the afternoon of the event found me relaxing on the edge of the swimming pool, with my feet in the water, sipping a glass of some very nice wine from Sofia's cellar.

Sofia and Miriam busied themselves with the food while Edward and some older boys set up a sound system. Jeff had his guitar out, too. We were going to have music, and, most certainly, dancing.

The younger children played with Annabel's toys. Annabel herself sat on Mary's lap, with two of her little friends on either side. It was an idyllic sight, black and white getting on together, perfectly.

However, Mary almost certainly had HIV. I wondered how long would she stay well. How long would it be before we, too, would share the experience that no African escaped: the premature death of someone you knew well? And how many of the others around us that day were also HIV positive?

But this was not a time to dwell on such sadness. Yes, I would have to be careful about Annabel's safety. But at least, there was one less thing I needed to worry about. Annabel could swim now.

I should not have been as surprised as I was to discover it. Since my fright at finding her practically unsupervised in the pool during our first week, I had resolved that she should quickly learn to swim, and I had only half-inflated her armbands ever since. She had been in the pool every day, but I had been so wrapped up in my own concerns, that I had failed to notice her growing confidence in the water. So I was taken aback completely when one day she announced she didn't need her armbands anymore, then jumped in and swam without them.

My eyes wandered over to where Faith, Hope and Charity were chatting up Livingstone and Jared. The two young doctors had returned from their holiday. I thought the girls might be wasting their time on the two men I suspected were gay. There again, if it was true, they would probably not be able to come out, such was the intolerance of homosexuality in these parts, and they might even have to get married to maintain a façade of normality.

My eyes slid over to the other side of the compound. Philippe had emerged from his house with Camelia on his arm. Was there a fairytale ending, here, for the family of orphans she had to provide for? On the other hand, perhaps a little clothes-mending business might stand them in better stead. Her sister, Salome, had learned to sew, and I nurtured hopes for her.

Loud laughter erupted from a corner where Thomas, Roy and Jeff were engrossed in a fierce debate, no doubt, about hospital affairs. '*Hakuna matata* – don't worry,' Thomas shouted, slapping Roy's shoulder.

There were plenty of things for Roy, and everyone else, to worry about, but today was not the time. I turned round and catching Thomas's eye, I raised my glass to him. *Hakuna matata* to you, too.

A little girl came up to me and took my hand. 'Mama Annabel,' she said. Her utterance had no verb; it was just a statement of who I was.

Who was I, and why was I was here? I had stopped asking myself that.

For a few seconds, I thought of what it would be like back in London on a drab, grey day in February, but I didn't want to dwell on it. For the next two years my home was here in Africa.

With all its gravity, this massive continent had pulled me towards itself. It was blighted with poverty, disease, conflict and exploitation, yet it had remained resilient, strong, warm, and exuberant. Africa: it was a mother of a continent. Well, it was *the* mother continent, because wasn't it in Rift Valley, not far from here, that humanity began? Africa had nurtured us. We had milked her and fed on her, and shown little gratitude.

Yet her people had opened her arms to Jeff and me. 'Welcome to Africa, Mrs Whitelady,' they had said.

I had my answer now. 'Thank you. I appreciate your hospitality.'

****

Coming soon

Nlimbo Fever

Granville Richardson

Anton Pilger is excited. He has finally arrived in the epicentre of his world, the Great Rift Valley in Africa, from where came the terrifying disease, Nlimbo Fever. Anton, who has been studying this disease for six years hopes to play a part in rescuing humankind from oblivion.

***

Blue Lagoons
and other stories

Julie Telford

Tales of hopes, dreams and disillusionment, yet sometimes emerging from the black clouds, a slither of silver.

***

Lightning Source UK Ltd.
Milton Keynes UK
UKOW040441311012

201452UK00001B/16/P